I0608414

FOREVER
CHRISTMAS

DEANNA ROY

casey shay press

Forever Christmas

Copyright © 2017 by Deanna Roy. All rights reserved.

No part of this book may be used or reproduced by any means, graphic, electronic, or mechanical, including photocopying, taping, and recording without written permission except in the case of brief quotations embodied in critical articles and reviews.

This is a work of fiction. All the characters, organizations, and events portrayed in this novel are either products of the author's imagination or used fictitiously.

Casey Shay Press
PO Box 160116
Austin, TX 78716
www.caseyshaypress.com

Paperback: ISBN: 9781938150739

Ebook-ISBN: 9781938150715

Library of Congress: Control Number: 2017957037

Other books by Deanna Roy

Forever Innocent
Part 1 of the Forever Series

Forever Loved
The shattering sequel to Forever Innocent

Forever Sheltered
Tina's story with Dr. Darion

Forever Bound
Jenny's story with songwriter Chance

Forever Family
The girls work toward their happily ever after

Stella & Dane
A bad boy romance

Baby Dust: A Novel about Miscarriage
Women's fiction on baby loss

Jinnie Wishmaker
Marcus Mender
an adventure series for 9-12 year olds under the name DD Roy

Learn more about the author at
www.deannaroy.com

For my rainbow babies

Emily
1999

Elizabeth
2002

Little Dude
adopted 2017

Go see all your rainbow baby dedications at the end of the book!

•*´`*•♥ •*´`*•

1

CORABELLE

It seems like every day lately is the first day of the rest of my life.

College. Graduation. Grad school. My first teaching assistant position.

But this one is just as big.

A nurse leads Gavin down the hall to an exam room. I follow, a little slowly, looking at the giant quotes painted directly on the walls.

If opportunity doesn't knock, build a door.

Instead of IMpossible, believe that I'M possible.

I hope it's all true.

We enter a room. A frigid blast of air-conditioning makes me shiver.

"Why is it always so cold here?" I whisper to Gavin.

"Maybe they want our balls to shrivel before they get all up in them," he says.

"Gavin!"

He laughs, and I'm glad he can be happy right now. I'm trying not to completely and utterly freak out.

All around us, wall-sized cork boards are lined edge to edge with photographs of babies. Some of them have just been born, a happy father in paper scrubs holding up the red-faced infant. Others simply show the babies, cherubic and precious on their fancy birth announcements. A few depict the whole family.

But mostly, the focus is on the fathers.

Fathers who had their fertility restored after reversing their vasectomies.

Fathers like Gavin.

Of course there are no pictures of the men who aren't successful. The ones who won't be holding a squalling baby. Who regret their choices. Whose marriages may be strained. Who may argue over adoption and donor sperm and the legalities of all the other options.

Or who choose to be childless.

That might be us.

Today we find out.

"We're surrounded," Gavin jokes as he hops up on the exam table. His voice isn't quite as jovial now. I think he's a little unnerved by the pictures too. The last room didn't have them. I wonder if it's a sign. They put you in the baby room if the reversal worked, a plain one if it didn't.

"I'm just going to take your vitals," the nurse says to Gavin, her voice curt and to the point. She has all the bedside manner of a billy goat.

I watch her strap a little device to Gavin's wrist. She cocks her hip in the pale green scrubs like this is all too much trouble. She's slight, small boned, pale skinned, fair haired. Her attitude makes up for her tiny size.

The little box beeps and she takes it off him.

"Am I dead?" Gavin asks.

She is not amused. "Vitals are fine," she says as she turns away. "The doc will be here in a second."

The door closes behind her.

"She can't thaw out," Gavin says. "It's the refrigerated rooms."

This makes me smile. "Maybe it's to control the man meat."

"I knew I was nothing more to you than a hot lay." He returns the smile, and I start to feel a little better. No matter what happens today, we're in this together.

"It makes up for your terrible fashion sense," I tell him.

He kicks his legs out, examining his work boots. There are oil smudges on his shirt, right under the little patch that reads "Gavin."

"It's weird for me to be the one on the table," he says.

"Hopefully it will be me next," I say, looking around at all the pictures.

"I thought we were going to wait," he says. "Until you're through grad school."

"I know." My eyes fall on one baby face, then another. That IS what we decided. To do the reversal surgery now, while we had the money, gifted to us from Tina's artist friend in his will. And while Gavin was still young. By the time we could afford a child, his chance of a successful reversal would be lower.

Money is an issue. We are behind on everything. I finished my undergraduate degree without scholarship help and am up to my eyeballs in student loans. And I'm only halfway through my master's degree. Gavin has to take classes slowly since he puts in so many hours at the garage.

I do have a teaching assistant position, which will help me achieve my dream of teaching college later on. But it doesn't pay much. We'll continue to get behind. Life is hard, but headed the right direction.

And now this.

Two swift knocks on the door are followed by the doctor peering in. He's the polar opposite of his nurse, all smiles and friendly handshakes. He is tall and lean, casual in jeans and a pale blue button-down beneath his open white lab coat.

"Gavin," he says. "Good to see you. Sounds like your recovery went fine."

"Used an ice pack or two, but things seem to be in working order." Gavin flashes a glance at me and even though I'm his wife, my face heats up.

"Good, good," the doctor says. My mind is blanking on his name. It doesn't matter. What he says is more important than who he is right now.

He pulls up a stool. "Let's talk about the results of the sample you gave us last week."

My face flames again. There are few things as awkward as helping your husband generate a sperm sample for a cup.

"We're three months out, so we should start seeing swimmers in there," the doctor says.

I'm bracing myself for the next part, where he says there aren't any. I'm so sure he will say this that I actually hear it, so when the doctor goes on, I'm momentarily disoriented when his words don't match my head.

"We are seeing activity now, which is good, really good." He nods at both of us. "But the count is low. Right on the cusp of what could reliably create a conception."

Gavin lets out a long stream of air. "So what's next?"

"We'll retest in another three months," he says. "Are you planning to conceive right away?"

"No," Gavin says, then turns to me for confirmation. I nod. "Is there anything we can do to help it?"

"Not necessarily for the count, but if it stays low, certainly we can wash the sperm, get the concentration up, and then do an insertion. It's not unusual to need this after a reversal."

Gavin's eyes look like they are going to pop out of his head. "Who would insert it?"

The doctor chuckles. "Your wife's obstetrician," he says. "It's a fairly simple procedure."

"And expensive," Gavin grumbles.

"Altering the path you chose early on isn't easy," the doctor says. "I'm glad to see that we've made progress, though." He stands and pats Gavin's shoulder. "You two are young. You'll get there."

"Thank you," I say.

He does another round of handshakes, then he's out the door.

Gavin jumps off the table. "Not bad news," he says.

"No, not the worst."

He extends his hand, and I take it. It's warm and strong and just holding it makes me feel better. This is Gavin, the boy I've known since I was a baby. Who crossed the alley behind our houses and slipped inside my fence from the time he could walk.

We're on the path to undoing the damage he did when he was eighteen and angry at the world, screwing over fatherhood because it had screwed him.

We walk back down the hall, past the nurses' station, to the checkout. While he makes his next appointment, I spot one more quote on the wall by the door.

Keep your face to the sunshine, and the shadows will fall behind you.

2

GAVIN

Despite the decent news, Corabelle definitely doesn't seem to be doing too well after the doc visit.

"I don't have to go back to Bud's," I tell her. "Why don't we do something together today?" We approach my motorcycle and I unlock our helmets. "There's a rock in the desert with our name on it."

Corabelle peers up at the sun. Summer is approaching, and the morning coolness has mostly burned off. San Diego isn't one for blazing temperatures, although the desert will certainly be warm.

"I'm not sure I'm dressed for a desert rock," she says, gesturing to her jeans and long-sleeved shirt.

"Where we're going, we don't need clothes," I say with a wink.

This gets her attention. Her eyebrows lift. "We should make a snack stop on the way. At least for water."

She's on board.

"Ever practical," I say, slinging a leg over the bike and waiting for her to settle in behind me. I hide my relief, as if I knew all along that she would come. "I could stand to melt some chocolate on your belly, though."

This gets a small laugh. "Sounds messy," she says.

"All the better to lick you."

Now the bigger laugh.

This is working.

I fire up the bike and we take off like a jet from the parking lot, the gloomy building, and the freeze-dried nurse.

I'm more conscious than usual, though, of my crotch, the vibrations of the motor. Did this help or hurt my sperm count? I should have asked. I didn't really ask any questions at all.

Pictures of my insides fill my head. Cartoon squigglies with long pointy tails, bumping around and popping like balloons until only a few remain.

I wash cold with the idea. Damn, I need to ditch that image.

I focus on the city passing by in a blur. Buildings. Trees. We get on the highway and zip alongside cars. Gradually, my buzzing head starts to get quiet. I can see the mountains in the distance, the red-brown of the desert hills before it.

The landscape gets quieter, the streets fewer and farther apart. We approach a gas station and Corabelle taps my arm. I pull in.

"I'll go," she says. "You stay with the bike."

She's always worried about losing the few things we have. I want to keep things easy today. Corabelle's way, no questions asked.

She's only inside a minute, coming out with bottles of water and a bag of trail mix. She holds up a bar of chocolate. That's my girl. She unzips the cargo bag attached to the back of the seat and sticks everything inside.

Then we're off again, into the desert, the air drying out. Traffic all but disappears, midmorning on a workday, and it feels like the entire world is ours.

I know where I want to take her. It's a spot we went to early on, when we first found each other again in astronomy class.

My gut tightens, just thinking about how close we came to spending our entire lives apart.

Our history is long, going back to childhood, my parents' house across the back alley. Corabelle was my first love, my only love, and we were inseparable even as toddlers. She saved me from my father. He wouldn't lay a hand on me in front of her. So I practically lived at her house.

Then high school came and she got pregnant. The town helped us out with a place to live. We had plans to do college part-time with her parents' help watching the baby.

Then Finn arrived two months early and with a heart condition. He lived seven days in the NICU.

My actions after that are not something I'm proud of. I blew up at Finn's funeral and ended up walking out. At the time I was nothing but anger, frustration, and guilt. I got it in my head that the world had decided I should never be a father. So I drove my car to Mexico and tracked down a clinic willing to do the vasectomy no questions asked, happy for the cash in US dollars.

That's what got me where we are now, trying to right the wrong, change our fate. I never thought I'd see Corabelle again, much less become her husband.

I aim to deserve her.

The reversal was a first step. There is nothing I won't do to make her happy.

We ride out, surrounded by nothing but dirt and rock and the occasional scrub brush. The highway cuts through like a streak of silver, the center stripe worn down by dust and time.

We pass Alpine, and I turn off the highway to cut down a dirt road. The terrain is rough and Corabelle holds on more tightly as we bump over ruts and ridges.

"I remember this part!" she yells next to my ear.

It's not far to the turn that leads to the plateau we visited before. It's been two years since the night we came here to do an astronomy project. It was a key night, part of our reconnection after Corabelle transferred to San Diego to finish her degree.

She hadn't known I was here, even though we'd both applied our senior year of high school, before she got pregnant. The plan changed with Finn and we chose New Mexico to be near her folks.

After Finn, Corabelle had stayed on in New Mexico. I'd burned that bridge by leaving, so I took up at the only other school to accept me.

I never dreamed we'd meet up again, and even though Corabelle had wanted nothing to do with me at first, I'd gradually convinced her to give me another chance.

The night on the rock had been part of that, and I hoped today would be another great memory.

We ride to the walking path, the motor revving to take on the incline. We're in the foothills now, a wind tunnel shaping the land into its own brand of art, statues made of dust and rock.

Brush has overgrown the path more than the last time we were here, so I have to stop the bike sooner. I kill the motor and

Corabelle sighs, stretching as she dismounts. "I'm not sure I'm in any better motorcycle shape than the last time we came here," she says.

It's true we only take short jaunts on the bike these days, preferring her car for anything more than a quick ride. But it makes my commute cheaper and the insurance break helps.

"Full body massage coming up," I say.

She shakes her head as she unloads the snacks, but I know that smile. She's with me. It's going to be a good afternoon.

The sun is bright white overhead. The mountains are pearl gray on the horizon, the sandblasted world around us a burnished red in the searing light.

"About as hot as I expected," I say and unlatch the rolled-up blanket from the side of the bike. We tramp around the brush, jumping on rocks and picking our way back to the path. I see the plateau ahead, a wide flat space among the hills and valleys.

I scramble up the embankment, then turn to help Corabelle. It feels like the last time, all nerves and anticipation. But right. We're together. No matter what else happens, we have that.

And this time she's my wife.

We straighten the blanket and lie back, closing our eyes to the blazing sky.

"Remember what happened last time we were here?" she asks.

"Why do you think I brought you?" I joke. "I'm aiming for a repeat."

Her arm flings out to bop my chest. "We'll get to that," she says. "We talked about Finn. The stars were out. They always reminded us of him."

"Still do," I say.

"True. I think this wide open space does it, though. Even without the stars."

I turn on my side to look at her. Beyond her the mountains and rock and wild brush spread out as far as you can see. We could be the only two people in the world. "You doing okay with the news this morning?" I ask.

"It's hopeful," she says. "Not the best, but not the worst either. Like life."

I prop my head on my hand and trail my fingers along the buttons down the front of her shirt. "Maybe the test in three months will be better."

She shifts on the blanket. It's a subtle movement, like she's trying to find a more comfortable spot. But I know her. It's not her body that is unsettled, but her heart.

"You don't think it will be?" I ask.

"No, I do," she says quickly, then bites her lip.

"What is it, then?"

"Jenny. And now Tina."

"Your friends?"

She doesn't answer, her eyes closed, and flings an arm over her face.

"Hey," I say. "Are they being all smug?"

Jenny just had a baby five months ago. Tina is expecting one in the fall.

"No, no. Of course not," she says. "It's just, oh, I don't know. Stressful."

"Because they have babies?"

"No. Yes."

Her throat works, swallowing hard. "Jenny had such a breeze, well, other than that crazy ambulance ride. And Tina is out of the woods. The cerclage is working perfectly."

"Still hard for her, though." Tina lost her baby to premature labor when she was a teenager as well. It took her years to recover.

"I know. I do. I get it. But at least they get that chance."

"We'll get it too. I know we will."

"When?" Her voice is high pitched and full of tears. "Two years from now, when I'm out of grad school? Or the day after never, because we'll be in debt forever?"

Her words drive a stake in my heart. "I'm graduating in a year. I'll get a great job and we'll do better."

She moves her arm so I can see her eyes. "You think so?"

"Sure."

I'd move heaven and earth to make that happen.

"In geology?"

"I've been talking to the placement department. I can work for consulting firms, especially around here."

I don't say that my chances would be better if I got my master's degree, but I can get started.

Corabelle goes quiet. I wonder if I've ruined things after all, if my stupid choice in Mexico will follow me all my life.

"Are you going to forgive me for all this?" I've asked before, a dozen times, maybe more. But I feel as though I need to keep asking, over and over, at least until we can build a family again.

She squints as she looks at me. I shift so that I shield her face from the sun.

"I forgave you a long time ago," she says. "Every time you ask, the answer will always be the same."

She turns to me then, pressing her palm against my chest. "You matter more to me than anything else."

Even though I know this is what she will say, what she will always say, relief still washes over me.

"I love you, Corabelle," I tell her.

She moves her hand to my cheek. "And I love you."

I think about making a joke about the melting chocolate, but her face is so earnest, so fragile, that instead I lean down to kiss her.

She accepts it, her lips parting slightly.

I know her. She's all I've ever really known. Her mouth. Her body. Her responses. She is everything. I have literally no recollection of anyone else. We were always meant to be. The four years we spent apart simply disappear, off in the distance, lost and forgotten. A blip in the passage of time. Not even a centimeter eroded on the landscape around us while we went through all that.

As if the universe has heard my thoughts, the wind kicks up and the sun slides behind a cloud, giving us a break and a cooling breath.

My hand moves to her buttons again and slowly, carefully, I release each one.

When my fingers cup her breast, she sighs against my mouth. I have her now. She is my Corabelle, my love. I shift over her, releasing her mouth to make my way down her jaw, her neck, her delicate collarbone, then the swell above the lace of her bra.

I slide my hand beneath her back, reaching for the clasp. It lets go, and I tug on the lace with my teeth. My mouth closes over the warm swollen nipple, and she arches up to meet me.

She is mine. I move more swiftly now, bracing on my elbow and moving my hand out from behind her to pluck open the snap to her jeans.

I know what she needs. I tug them down, the denim sliding over her hips. Her panties are soft blue and simple. I already knew this. I pretty much always watch her dress in the morning. It's one of the best parts of my day.

We are not often out naked on a bright day like this, and the tiny lightning bolts of her stretch marks are prominent across her belly. She is no longer shy about them. I kiss each one, tracing their path down her abdomen. The evidence of Finn. I think of him every time.

She kicks her heels against the rock to knock off her shoes. One flies away and rolls off our plateau. I'll fetch it later. I pull her jeans all the way off, my lips still pressing against her bare stomach.

When I've got her legs free, I part her knees and fit myself between her calves. My fingers flirt with the edges of the panties. She sucks in a breath. She knows where I'm headed.

I tug on the soft fabric, exposing her hip, then the first flirty hint of downy hair. I make my way farther down, taking the panties with me as I go.

When they've cleared her ankles, I lean in, gently sweeping my tongue against all my favorite spots. She lets out a soft sigh, her hands grabbing the edges of the blanket.

I'm done with gentle now, diving in and using all my knowledge of her to my advantage. Corabelle cries out, spreading wide, her voice echoing off the walls of the canyon.

Her hands bury themselves in my hair. I add fingers, moving faster, and I know right when she loses it, pulsing against me, her voice rising.

I bring her down carefully, massaging her thighs. Sometimes

after an emotional day, being together like this can set her on an emotional spiral. She flings her arm over her face, but after only a moment, she recovers and sits up.

Her hands reach for my shirt, pulling all the snaps apart in a single swift motion.

Oh, this girl.

I toss the shirt as she reaches for my jeans. I have to pause to unstring my boots, and in my hurry to set them aside, one of my boots joins her shoe off the edge. We both laugh as I wrap my arms around her waist.

"You going to give me sore knees?" she asks. "Again?"

"I'll do my best." I roll up the side edges of the blanket as a cushion for her. "How's that?"

"Good enough," she says, bringing her leg up and over me as easily as she did the motorcycle.

I picture her riding my bike naked, and I'm so hard I feel like I could break the rock we're lying on.

She settles her knees, then shifts her body over mine.

It's like sliding into bliss. The sun shines down on her, as brightly as if we were riding one of its rays. She's beautiful, like a goddess, and it's not hard to imagine that the light comes from her and not the other way around.

She moves over me, knowing me just as well as I do her.

We fit. Always did. From that very first time in her parents' sunroom to that sweet beautiful night in her apartment after we found each other again.

And now, we glow as if the world wants to pour all its beauty into one spot for the day.

She rocks against me, her eyes closed. Her breasts sway over me and I can barely hold anything in. When I feel her movements get more deliberate, I grasp her hips and increase the pressure, the intensity, the drive.

She loses it again, leaning over me, her voice in my ear. I release into her, pulsing with the bliss, overwhelmed by how she lets go, how she loves me, how we are together.

Her body flattens against mine, her head on my chest. My fingers trace her skin. My Corabelle. We stay like this for long minutes, time dropping away like the trickles of water in a cavern.

Only later, when we've dressed and I've hopped down on one foot to retrieve our errant shoes, do I realize we haven't used condoms since I told her about the vasectomy.

But we might want to think about them now.

3

CORABELLE

The end of the second quarter arrives. Jenny and I start repurposing decorations from her baby shower for Tina's wedding. Even though Tina's marrying a doctor and they could do pretty much anything, they've decided to keep it small and informal. We're prettying up a small arch to put on a cliff that is important to them.

On the last day of class, my American Lit professor calls me to his office. I've been his teaching assistant this last year, and loved every minute of it.

Professor White is great. He's supported me doubling up on classes so I can get through my master's sooner. I'm hoping to start work on my doctorate next year and maybe score a better-paid adjunct position so I can start pummeling at my student loans. The TA stipend isn't much, although I'm grateful to be doing it rather than working at the old coffee shop like I used to.

When I peek through his open door, Professor White is

sitting behind his desk. The surface is littered with papers, and a rather unstable stack of books leans unsteadily on one corner.

"Corabelle!" he says, standing. His dress shirt is wrinkled, as always, and his belt is way too long, the end hanging down to his thigh. Apparently he used to weigh twice what he does now, and he keeps the belt to remind him of where he's been.

But his eyes are merry, and the new beard he's growing to be fashionable is still scraggly and sparse.

"What's up?" I ask, dropping my overloaded backpack to the ground and settling on the hardback chair opposite his desk.

"I guess you know Theresa is graduating in December," he says. Theresa is one of the adjunct professors he supervises. "She's gotten a position in New York."

"That's great!" I say. "She's worked hard for it."

"She has. I saw you are within striking distance of completing your master's. Are you closing in on your thesis?"

My heart hammers. "I am."

"I've really liked your work. Both your help as a TA and your graduate papers. Real standout stuff." He opens a desk drawer. "I kept this one." He places a stapled set of pages on the pile in front of him.

I recognize it. My paper on Dante's *Inferno*. I'd probably gotten a little too personal in it, comparing some of my experiences to his infamous Circles of Hell.

"Tapping into your own life story to bring a unique interpretation to a work is what literature is all about," he says. "So, I'm relieving you as my TA."

My body goes cold. He's firing me?

"What?" I ask, my voice shaking.

"I want you in a better position to become an adjunct when Theresa leaves. If you're under contract for the academic year as my TA, you can't easily shift over."

It takes a moment for the words to sink in. If I'm a TA, I can't be an adjunct when it's time. This is a good thing.

"Really? So soon?" I ask.

"Will you complete your work and your thesis by December?"

I think fast. It's seven months away. "I can, as long as I take an extra class third quarter."

"Good, consider it done. You could probably use the break from TA duties while you hammer that thesis out anyway."

I frown. "But I'll lose the stipend."

It isn't much, but it's something. I'll have to pick up shifts at Cool Beans, if they'll take me back. Or get some other job. We run too close on bills to lose that money.

"I'll handle that. They haven't selected scholarship recipients for fall quarter yet. I'll make sure they make up that pay."

"You will?"

He smiles. "Absolutely."

I sit back in the chair. It's what I've wanted forever. To move through my teaching experience so I could become a professor. Adjunct is the next step. It's the best possible scenario.

Except.

I want a baby.

After our desert rock moment, Gavin and I agreed that we wouldn't buy condoms after all, and I wouldn't get on the pill. If there wasn't enough sperm, there wasn't enough. If something happened, it was meant to be.

But, here was this position.

If I got pregnant, the whole plan would collapse.

"Corabelle?"

I snap back to Professor White.

"What is your concentration?" he asks.

"North American Lit," I say quickly.

"Good, good," he says. "I'll get that scholarship application to you." He stands up. "I've never had more pleasure in firing someone."

I pick up my backpack. "I've never been so happy to get fired. Thank you. I can't wait." I'm gushing, but my mind is elsewhere. I have to tell Gavin I've changed my mind.

"You okay, Corabelle?" Professor White asks.

"Sure, yes, of course," I say. I need to get out of here before I blow this. "Thank you!"

I hurry out, walking quickly down the hall and out of the building. My breathing is labored, and I suck in air. Did I just give up on having a baby? What did that mean?

The quad is quiet. I find a bench and sit down. I miss Jenny being here on campus with me, but she graduated a year ago. I haven't made a friend like her on campus since I started my graduate coursework. It's different. Everyone is focused and often juggling work and school, sometimes family too.

Family. What I don't have. Won't have.

Might never have.

My mind whirs. I can't quite assimilate this new version of my future against what we had just decided. I want to rationalize why I don't want a baby right now after all. Convince myself I'm making the right choice.

Would a baby even happen if I gave up this opportunity?

Gavin's sperm count is low. And even if it wasn't, I don't know how likely it would be that another baby would have a heart defect.

Mom had four miscarriages. Why? Did those babies have bad hearts? Finn's condition could be genetic. Or it could be environmental. Or just bad luck.

I hadn't had a reason to think on pregnancy for a long time. It only just now became possible again.

A little bit possible. Or, at least, not *im*possible.

I'm possible.

I breathe deeply, trying to relax. I'm spiraling back into my old thinking, my old worries. I have a real thing going here. A real chance.

The job I've always wanted. The opportunity I've waited for.

A chance to move on.

It isn't time for babies.

When I get to my car, instead of heading for home, I stop by a pharmacy and pick up a big box of condoms. Sixty count. Gavin will think it's great.

At home, I head into the bathroom and move aside my boxes of tampons to unbury the ovulation kit I bought a few weeks ago, when I learned Tina was coming home to marry Darion and have their baby.

The machine is heavy in my hand. So recently I had held that hope close to my heart. It was a wonderful hope — the idea that I would have my baby too, and we three friends would raise our children together.

Instead, I will focus on teaching and learning. There will be time for babies, but it isn't now.

I could return the ovulation computer. We could use the money. By the time I might use it, the little sticks that go inside would be expired.

But I can't quite do it. I need to keep this hope in my house.

I bend down to peer into the cabinet. In the very back are things we rarely use. Old towels. An electric razor that doesn't hold a charge. Pink sponge rollers my mother insisted I should keep.

I shove the box to the back with those items. Gavin said he would get a new job in a year. By then, I'd be an adjunct professor working on my Ph.D. We'd both make real money, get out of debt.

Everything was working out.

A family could wait.

4

GAVIN

Jenny and Corabelle spend a lot of time together making sure Tina's wedding will be nice, since Tina isn't crazy about the whole production.

I take the opportunity to work extra hours at Bud's. I want to take Corabelle somewhere nice to celebrate the adjunct job. I'm so proud of her. She'll be teaching her own class pretty much the moment she has her master's.

I don't have those sorts of aspirations. I like working at Bud's. It's steady work and I'm friends with the people there. I know I'll have to figure out the next step when I get my degree, but that seems far off still. Corabelle deciding the baby should wait after all has taken the pressure off.

The stacks of old worn tires are three deep in the back room and getting in the way, so I volunteer to load them into the recycling bin. It's a real chore, rolling or lugging them out behind the shop and pitching them into the metal bin that gets picked up every month.

The task is below my pay grade, and I should be making Barry, the garage grunt, do it. But I haven't had as much time to lift weights since I moved in with Corabelle, and tossing tires is pretty much the best workout you can get paid for.

The garage is quieter than usual, so I've got time to step away from the mechanic bays. The sun beams down, and I feel pretty fine as I flex and let another tire fly over the rim of the bin to land with a thud inside.

My phone buzzes. I tug it out of my pocket. It's Corabelle. Wonder what she's up to? She's supposed to be with Jenny.

She sounds a little upset as she asks, "Did you hear from Rosa?"

It's not her favorite topic. Rosa is the mother of Manuel, a little boy she raised without telling me he was mine. She's from Mexico. I was too stupid back then to know my vasectomy didn't work right away.

"Yes," I tell her. "Looks like we're on for June. Just in time for Tina's wedding."

Her next words don't quite match her tone. I can tell she's distraught over something. "I'm so glad, Gavin. It will be good to see him."

"Are you okay, Corabelle?" I ask. I'm not sure if this is about Rosa or if it's been hard for her to be around Jenny's baby. I can hear her friend calling to her in the background.

"Hold on, Gavin, Jenny's running at me. We've been making Tina's wedding stars," she says.

I listen in as she asks Jenny what's going on.

I can't hear what Jenny responds.

The sun bears down on me. The air smells of tires and asphalt and oil.

Corabelle's breath changes, her breathing hard.

"Corabelle," I say. "Everything okay?" I know it's not, but I'm not sure what I can do. I start walking to the shop to tell Bud I'm leaving. I think Corabelle needs me.

She doesn't answer, so I poke my head through the opening to the pit. "Mario, can you sign me out? I've got to go."

He nods. I was an extra on hand today anyway.

Bud comes out in his overalls, wiping his hands on a towel. "You all right?" he asks.

"Not sure," I say and just walk away. I can clue them in later. Once I know myself. I keep the phone pressed to my ear. "Corabelle, are you at Jenny's? I'll come get you."

"No," she finally says. "I mean, yes, you should come, but you don't need to get me."

I'm so relieved to hear her say something finally. "What's going on, baby? Can you tell me?"

She hesitates, then says. "I took a pregnancy test. Jenny had one. Leftover. We were just being silly."

My heart thuds. She wouldn't mention this unless it was important. Still, I have to ask. "How did it turn out?"

I flash back to that day, so many years ago, when she peed on the stick in the bathroom of her parents' house. We were teens. Scared. But we decided we could do it. We'd make it work.

"It's positive, Gavin. We already did it. It's already there."

Thankfully, there's a bench three steps away, so I sit on it.

For a moment, my head is just empty, like all my thoughts

26

flew out. Then the cartoon sperm fill my head, wiggling around, flexing their biceps. So much for doctors. We'd been using condoms for a few weeks, so it had to be that first day, on the rock.

We were about to do everything all over again. I don't know if she's happy about it or not, given the job. Given Finn.

"You feeling okay?" I ask her.

"I think so."

"You scared?" I ask.

"Petrified." She gives a shaky laugh.

"Me too," I say. My brain is bringing up scenes from the past like my life is flashing before my eyes. Corabelle at her parents' house. The test. Her belly swelling. Her water breaking. The hospital. The incubator. The funeral.

I grip the arm of the bench. The metal is hot but I don't let go. It's reality. It grounds me.

"We're going to have a baby, Gavin," she says. I can hear the tears in her voice.

"We are, we really are," I say. My own voice cracks. So much to think about. I can barely hold it all in.

"I'm coming over," I say to her. "Stay right where you are."

"Okay," Corabelle says. "I'll be waiting for you. We both will. Me and this baby."

I remember all the pictures we looked at the first time, the kidney bean turning into a shrimp, then a miniature baby, then a balled-up infant barely fitting in the tight space. All that had already begun.

Life sure is turning on a dime lately.

And here we go again.

5

CORABELLE

I don't know what to do with myself.

Gavin is at work. I have a one-week break between classes.

I'm no longer a TA, so no prep work to do.

And I'm pregnant.

I keep saying it over and over again.

I'm pregnant.

I'm pregnant.

The bathroom mirror reflects my image back at me. I am the same Corabelle. Long dark hair, pale face, faded T-shirt, jeans that won't fit much longer.

But I'm more. I press my hands against my belly. Someone is in there. Another boy? My heart squeezes, remembering Finn's tiny face.

Or a girl this time? Like Jenny's little Phoenix or the one soon to be born to Tina?

I don't know what I want. Other than no heart defect. No premature labor.

No hospitals, wires, breathing tubes, or NICU.

Maybe I am asking too much. The pregnancy is a miracle all by itself.

I called Jenny's ob/gyn since I didn't really think the health center at the university was the right place to go. The woman who schedules appointments said to come in at nine weeks when we could do a sonogram, but if I was worried to come in sooner.

I like that I'm welcome to check in with them anytime. But that doesn't keep me from being scared out of my mind.

My professor is out of town for the summer, and the quick email I sent him saying I might have to change my plans got an automatic out-of-office reply. The baby is due in February, which means I would take maternity leave only six weeks into the new position as an adjunct professor.

I'm going to have to turn the dream job down.

I should finish my master's degree before my due date, though, as long as everything goes well.

It has to go well.

Otherwise I'll have given up my opportunity for nothing.

Well, not for nothing. Finn was not nothing.

But for another baby I will not get to raise.

I can't think this way.

I shake it off and push away from the sink.

It's no use to buy into that negativity. I have to believe. I'm possible. The baby's possible. Our future is possible.

My bare feet are a whisper down the hall. The carpet in front of the sofa needs to be vacuumed, dirt brought in by Gavin's work boots. I think I see a few sparkles too, remnants from when I worked on Tina's stars before taking them over to Jenny's.

The closet door in the living room sticks when I try to open it, and I have to jerk it hard. The vacuum inside is probably a hundred years old. It was left in the apartment by a previous tenant but still works.

I can't quite roll it out due to all the junk in there, most of it Gavin's unused weight equipment. I have to shove aside a giant wheel marked fifty pounds. My arms protest the strain.

I feel a pull in my belly and a white-hot panic shoots through me. Did I do something already? I'm not supposed to lift heavy things.

Tears spring to my eyes as lightning bolts of pain trickle up my abdomen. I'm already doing everything wrong! How in the world am I supposed to get a healthy baby here?

My body bends over as I shuffle to the sofa and lie down. I breathe slowly in and out, assessing. What hurts? Is there anything wet down below? I picture blood and I'm horrified to actually feel it, wet and sticky.

I leap up, forgetting to be careful, and race to the bathroom. I remember Jenny calling me, hysterical, from a hotel room in Tennessee after she tracked down Chance. She was bleeding and sure she'd lost the baby.

Except Phoenix got here fine. I was the one to calm her down, assure her that a little blood was fairly common.

I jerk down my jeans in the bathroom, expecting to see an ocean of red.

But there's nothing. Absolutely nothing.

I imagined it.

I pull my pants back up and sit on the edge of the tub. This is terrible. My heart beats too fast and my stomach is a block of stone. How will I ever make it through nine months of this? How does anyone face a new pregnancy after the ultimate failure?

My baby had been damaged beyond repair. The doctors wouldn't even give him a chance, refusing the heart surgery he needed to survive. He lived and died in a hospital. I only held him when they took the breathing tubes away.

I don't move, my fingers gripping the edge of the tub, just trying to breathe. A lot of time passes, but it's only me at home. Nothing will pull me out of this spiral. I have to do it myself.

At last my chest loosens a little and I can take a breath deep enough to calm my anxiety. My back aches from my position, so I stand and head to the living room.

The old comfy armchair beckons. The arms are shredded and I've thrown hand towels over them. But it's broken in just right, and I sink into it like I'm collapsing into an embrace.

When I was in Houston with Tina a month ago, we retrieved the remains of her baby so that they could be cremated. Her old friend Stella walked the path of the cemetery with us. She ran a pregnancy loss group that Tina belonged to years ago, back when Peanut was born prematurely and lived only three hours.

Stella said that a new pregnancy after a loss is called a rainbow baby, the beauty after the storm. "You've survived the tempest," Stella said. "Now let yourself believe you will see the colors arcing across your sky."

I stare at the ceiling, willing myself to find hope. It seems terribly far away. I search my heart and head for that small comforting light and simply can't find it. I had a grip on it so recently, sitting in the office with Gavin, learning he had some sperm.

Certainly I felt it when I learned I would be an adjunct.

And then again, when Jenny ran out of her apartment with the pregnancy stick, telling me what I had not even guessed could be true.

But now with a single twinge of pain, it had fled.

The images of Finn hang on the wall opposite me. The incubators were thick clear plastic with the blue circles where you could place your hands inside. A gray mask covered his eyes, and a tube snaked into his mouth, taped down on both cheeks. So little skin even showed. He was all wires and plastic wrap and blinking lights.

I try to imagine going through all that again, and I can't summon the strength. My head collapses on the broad arm of the chair. This is too much for anybody.

I need Tina. She will understand how I feel. Of course, her pregnancy problem has a name. Incompetent cervix. So easy to take action for. A little wire around her cervix keeps the baby from sliding out too early. But does she feel safe? Is she able to nurture that little light of hope?

My hand reaches out to the coffee table for my phone. Tina is already five months pregnant, almost precisely the point when her Peanut was born too early. We don't usually talk about these things, but I need to. I need her.

I have a feeling she needs me.

I text her a quick note, just about the wedding. If she's busy, I don't want to drop some big stress bomb on her in the middle of something important.

She writes back quickly, noncommittal about the decorations. She really doesn't care much about the aesthetics of her wedding, only the people and place. So I dive in.

I just hallucinated the feeling of blood, like I lost the baby. I don't how to stop it.

Her response is swift.

Coming over.

I wait in the chair, afraid to move, angry I lifted the weight, upset I'd felt the nonexistent blood. My body is betraying me, making things worse.

I've only known about the baby for a week. Would it get better? Or worse?

Time passes imperceptibly. The air conditioner kicks on and off and on again. The kitchen faucet drips. Cars pull into the parking lot of the apartment complex, doors slamming, footsteps crossing wood bridges to the units all around.

Then I hear the soft knock, as if Tina is afraid to wake me.

I stand slowly, like I'm one hundred years old, feeling the stiffness from holding my position too long out of fear.

When I pull the door open, Tina immediately steps into a hug. This is new. Tina is not a hugger.

She kicks the door closed, dropping us into semi-blackness. I hadn't realized I was living in the dark until I saw the light from a door.

Tina walks around, flipping switches and opening blinds. My eyes drop to her belly. She's tiny, so her belly bump is already quite pronounced. She hasn't bought any proper maternity clothes, so her shirt is stretched to the max above a broomstick skirt and delicate ballet flats.

Her usual twiggy blond ponytails coming off the back of her head are longer and fuller. Pregnancy makes your hair thicker.

I touch mine. It's too early for me to notice that effect yet.

"So tell me about the blood," Tina says, her voice no nonsense. She drops onto the sofa, tossing her keys on the coffee table.

"There wasn't any," I say. "I just felt it suddenly. I absolutely knew it was there. But it was nothing."

"All in your head," she says wryly, looking behind me at the wall. Finn's pictures are there. I figure that's what she sees. "At least that's what male doctors say when women have female issues."

"My ob/gyn is really nice," I say. "He wouldn't say that."

Tina nods. "Mine is pretty great too. This time."

I wonder what her old doctor had said to her about her premature labor and losing a baby as a teen. Obviously something patronizing or diminishing. It was a common thing, and not just for pregnant mothers. All women. When you found a good doctor, male or female, who cared enough to actually listen, you definitely held on.

She straightens her skirt. "Back when I was in a support group, one of the women, Melinda, hallucinated blood on the floor all the time. It's because she got blood all over her tile floor."

"That's terrible!" I exclaim, already feeling better about my situation compared to hers. "Did she have a baby?"

"Yeah, about a year later. She got pregnant again pretty fast."

"So it happens to others." I can't imagine seeing blood on the floor just randomly. Although it was definitely no better to feel it. But maybe now that it's happened once, I can control my panic the next time.

"How's the breathing thing?" she asks. Her eyes don't leave my face. She's not going to give me a pass on this issue. She knows I used to get so strung out that I would hold my breath until I went unconscious.

"I haven't done it in forever." My voice is serious, but firm so she knows I mean it. "I'm not going to hurt the baby by doing that."

"Good," she says. "It's okay to be worried. Even women who haven't lost a baby get paranoid."

Paranoid. Is that what I am? Probably.

"We won't be able to see the baby's heart clearly until I'm four months along," I tell her.

"That's long. What happens if this one has the problem?"

"I have no idea. They can't do anything to fix it until they are born. It's difficult surgery already."

"You look things up today? Is that what made you panic?"

"No, I moved one of Gavin's weights and had a pain."

She won't lecture me on lifting things. She knows that I'm aware of the rules. And that things happen. You forget. Or you have no choice. Or it just happens whether you play it safe or not.

"It's probably nothing. Did you call your doctor?"

I shake my head. "He's new and I haven't even seen him yet."

"Doesn't matter. You can call them before your first appointment."

I sit back down in the armchair. "I'm fine now, I guess. I'm more freaked out about feeling the blood than I am about the pain I had."

She nods. Her hand goes to her belly, then she catches herself and rests it on the sofa.

"How is your baby coming?" I ask.

"Everything is fine. Got the twist tie on."

"No premature labor pains?"

"Not so far. I hear it will be a bitch if it happens. Your body does not appreciate it if you thwart it from ejecting something it wants out."

"Will you go on bed rest if that happens?"

"Probably hospitalized, if we can't stop it. But generally it's the cervix failing that allows labor, not labor pushing on the weak cervix. So it should be fine."

This is a relief. "I'm glad."

"It's a simple thing," she says. "I just didn't know it before."

I imagine how different Tina's life would be if she hadn't lost Peanut, if she'd known to do a cerclage. I can't imagine being pregnant again, understanding that saving your first baby would have been so simple, if only you had known.

There was no way to have helped Finn.

But if he hadn't had the heart condition, I know exactly where I'd be, still with Gavin, still in New Mexico. Maybe one day, if we can get this new baby here safe and healthy, my life will shift back onto that rail.

"This isn't going to be easy," Tina says. "This time around, I ignored any sign I was pregnant for over a month, but once it kicks in, it consumes you."

Her face is serious, and I can see the tiredness in her now.

"But you're doing okay," I say.

She flattens her hands beneath her chin like she's taking one of those old Olan Mills portraits. "I make it look good, don't I?" she says, batting her eyes.

"But not so much inside," I finish.

Tina drops her hands and shrugs. "There's only so much angst and paranoia other people are willing to tolerate." She leans back against the cushions and stares up at my ceiling. "Darion's good," she says. "But pretty much everyone else, including our dear Jenny, seems to think I should be cherishing every moment."

She drops her chin and stares me right in the eye. "I just want this over. Baby here. Not dead. Doing normal baby things."

I flinch at the word *dead*. Tina doesn't mince words. Never has. She used to do a talking circuit about suicide. The cuts across both her wrists have long since healed, and only people who know about them can spot the pale pink welts where they once were.

My own history isn't a whole lot better. Such a long terrible fall we've both somehow managed to survive.

And here we are, right back into the fire.

We sit in silence for a while, keeping each other company. It's the most important thing right now. Just being. Especially when you're in the presence of someone who gets you all the way to the bone.

6

GAVIN

I think Corabelle is managing okay.

I watch her all the time, looking for signs that the strain is too much for her. But she does her Corabelle things. Dinner. Tidying. Reading. Studying.

I've been working extra hours at Bud's trying to get ahead on bills. Today I have to replace a radiator, which is a pain and a half. Twice Bud himself has come over so we can wrangle it out from the hoses and tight-set motor.

Right now I'm hooking the new one in.

I came home twice last week to find Tina sitting with Corabelle. Once they weren't even talking, just hanging out in the living room staring at the walls. Corabelle says she had a bit of a scare and Tina waited with her until she settled down.

The other time, they were painting rainbows on tall glass containers filled with candle wax. Corabelle has kept hers lit pretty much every moment since. She's never really been a rainbow person, but maybe it was Tina's idea.

I worry about her. But she's back in class for the summer quarter, her load considerably lighter just taking classes and not being a TA. Her prof came through with a scholarship even though Corabelle had to turn down the adjunct position. He's good like that. Corabelle was relieved as she felt like she needed to work at the coffee shop otherwise.

No way would I let that happen. I've taken the summer off from school to get more hours, and I could defer a semester. I'm already on the seven-year plan. Might as well go for ten.

We're both marking time now. I guess parents do. But it's not just the baby coming we count the days for. It's the mid-pregnancy sonogram. This time, they'll look at the baby's heart and see if it is developing correctly. It's not something they normally examine in a routine visit. But since Finn's heart defect could be genetic, we have to know.

My phone buzzes, but I have to ignore it. I've got both hands in the guts of this Mazda, making sure every hose is locked down and tight.

Mario walks by. "You got it?" he asks.

I nod and walk my hands along the radiator, making sure it sits correctly and none of the hoses are pinched.

When I'm free, I pick up my phone to see who called. I really hope it wasn't Corabelle with a problem.

It's not.

It's my mom's cell phone. She hasn't left a voice mail.

I don't talk to her very often, just Christmas and Mother's Day. I call my sister June on her birthday, though, and she sometimes calls me if she's by herself. She's fourteen.

I shove my phone back in my pocket. If it was important, Mom would have left a message. I head to the driver's side of the car to fire it up and let it run to make sure it doesn't overheat.

But my phone buzzes once more.

Mom again.

Something has to be going on, so this time I pick up.

"Hey," I say.

"Gavin? Is that you?" Her voice is tremulous and scared.

"It's me, Mom," I say, and my heart thuds when I hear how she sounds.

"I need you to come home," she says.

"Is June okay?"

She sniffles. "It's your father," she says. "He's having heart bypass surgery the day after tomorrow."

My body stills. I imagine my father dead and find I have zero concern about it. He's a bitter, angry, awful old man, and no one is going to mourn his death.

"Gavin? You still there?"

"I'm here. I heard you."

"Are you coming?"

I hesitate. "Nah. I've got a lot going on here."

"But he's your father. He might not make it through this."

"I quit considering him my father the last time he gave me a black eye," I say. "You and June still okay?"

"We are," she says. "He's changed, Gavin."

"I doubt that," I say. "But I'm glad he isn't hurting you."

I'd kill him if he did, but it was always about me. Never the girls.

I think about June. We don't talk about Dad. But he can't be good for her, even if he isn't one to punch a female.

"Please, Gavin. Make amends with him before the surgery."

"Is Grandma K there to help you?" I ask.

"Of course," she says.

"And Uncle Ben?"

"He's coming."

"Then sounds like you have plenty of help. Let me know if he keels over. I'll buy the first round."

"Gavin!"

"I'm serious, Mom. Love you."

And I end the call.

I do love her, and my sister. But if she thinks I'm going to drop everything and go play nicey nice with the man who bruised me body and soul, she's wrong.

Dead wrong.

I sit in the seat of the Mazda, watching the temperature gauge. It's holding steady, unlike the way I'm feeling inside.

"Everything all right?" Mario asks. He bends down, his head by the door. His hair is wild, black and curling. He hasn't cut it since his last girlfriend.

"Just parent stuff," I say. "Nothing important."

"Temp holding?" he asks.

"Looking good."

"Cool. Because some hot chick just drove in an engine overhaul, and I'm going to need a second set of hands."

"For the car or the chick?"

He elbows me. "Yeah, right. You won't even shoot pool with me. Bona fide househusband. Your bachelorhood is blown."

"I don't make a good wingman," I say.

"Yeah, they always want the married one anyway," he says. His fingers comb through the wild tangle on his head. "I'm thinking of growing my hair long, get a beard. That's the look now."

"Don't ask me for grooming advice. I barely remember to shave."

"The chicks seem to dig that look on you."

I shrug. This is one of the reasons I don't hang with Mario since Corabelle came back. He doesn't recognize that my priorities are completely rearranged.

"I'm going to bring her car around," he says. "Bay three."

"I'll be there in a sec," I tell him. I'll have one of the grunts take the Mazda for a drive to make sure it's all working.

I clear the tools from the area and drop the hood. A towel gets caught in the latch, and I have to lift it again to clear it. My head betrays me, flashing back to a morning a long time ago, working on Mom's car with Dad. He had me do that a lot, insisting I learn a trade.

I was probably ten or so. Normally Corabelle hung around when I was with Dad, as he wouldn't hit me when she was watching. He felt like the Rothefords were nosy and would call the cops even though he had every right to discipline his son. But that day Corabelle was shopping with her mom.

That morning I closed the hood on the shop towel, just like I did today. It shouldn't have been any big deal. It's just a crappy old rag, and lifting the hood a second time took all of five seconds.

But Dad was already frustrated and annoyed that he'd had to buy a new battery for the car. He blamed Mom for it, since she only ever drove to church and back, and he was sure those short trips were killing the alternator or the battery or both.

It was stupid, and we both knew it. He tried to make her walk instead, told her she could use the exercise anyway. This was his way of berating her, keeping her down. I only knew he was wrong because I practically lived at Corabelle's house, and I saw the way a man ought to treat his wife.

But I couldn't do anything about it.

I pulled the towel out and lowered the hood, hoping he wouldn't say anything about my mistake.

But of course he had. He snatched the towel from me and snapped it at my head. The corner whipped against my cheek, causing a sharp sting.

I turned away to pick up the tools, but he was just warming up.

"You can't do a single damn thing right the first time, can you, boy?" His voice had that low threatening quality I knew meant I better split fast. I could run, hide somewhere for the day, wait for Corabelle to come home. Most weekends I stayed over there until late, when I could sneak in, my father snoring on the recliner.

I dropped the wrench in the toolbox and headed past the car to the sidewalk. My father was strong but not fast. I could outrun him if I got a chance.

He knew it, stepping between me and the car. I was blocked.

I could go back through the garage into the house and cut through the kitchen. But he'd know I was running then. It would only make things worse later, tomorrow or whenever it caught up to me.

For some reason, that day I decided I was done running. I stared him right in the eye and stood up straight.

I would take this blow and move on.

His face was a sneer as I did my best to square my shoulders. We glowered at each other, seconds ticking. I waited for the blow. He didn't do it.

So I asked, "You want me to start it up?"

This caught him a bit by surprise. He expected me to cower, to run. He wiped the battery crud off his hands onto the towel. His squinty eyes took me in. "Yeah," he said. "See if you even connected it right."

No blow.

I scooted past him and he cuffed my head as I passed, but that was nothing. I climbed into Mom's car and turned the key. The engine hesitated, uneasy. But after a catch or two, it fired up.

My father stood there, frowning at the car, hands on his hips. He seemed less intimidating with the car between us. I could close the door and lock it. If I dared, I could put the car in reverse and just take off.

Or put it in drive and run him over.

But it was a big moment. I hadn't backed down.

The towel has reminded me of this moment, this knife-edge of wanting to be gone, or him dead.

Now I'm grown, and I'm gone, and he might die.

And by God, I simply can't find any sympathy in my heart.

7

CORABELLE

I might be spending too much time alone. My graduate courses are only a few hours a week and there's no office to hang out in on campus. Gavin works extra so we can find some way to pay for a baby.

My days are filled with studies and notes and plans for my thesis. Sometimes I sleep, finding midafternoons long and difficult now that I'm pregnant.

I haven't told Gavin about the dreams.

They come almost every night and sometimes during naps. Their intensity and vividness don't surprise me. I had them with Finn too, technicolor spectacles with majestic soundtracks and convoluted storylines. They felt so real that when I would awaken in the night, I had to roll over to Gavin and touch him to ensure that this dim silent world was the real one after all.

But those were mostly happy, silly, giddy, or strange.

Not these.

In the new version of my pregnancy dreams, I see the baby, floating in the watery world of my belly, red-tinged and ghostly. The view closes in on a precious face, tiny hands, and a round belly strung with its umbilical cord.

Then we're inside of him, his blood vessels, his lungs.

And his heart.

It beats oddly, lopsided, pulsing and pushing like a distorted accordion. Then a spring pops, and screws spew out. After a few more swollen beats, there's a little explosion and his heart becomes a gutted music box, bits of metal and wire hanging loose.

Every night, the same.

I've learned to dread it, even while I sleep. When the view starts to close in on his heart, I know what is coming. I fight the dream, trying to wake myself, shaking hard, knowing my body can't move. I want away from it, to avoid the journey inward. But there is no escape. Until the heart explodes to bits of machinery, I can't change the course.

Yesterday I wrote Stella, the baby loss support group leader who helped Tina. She's seen so many women, so many ways of grieving. I hoped she could tell me how to stop the dreams. I'm still waiting for a reply.

I have an hour until I have to leave for class. My comfy armchair cradles me. Gavin left for work early this morning, so like most days, I am alone.

My laptop glows softly in the cave-like room, shutters closed to keep out the heat and save money on air-conditioning. I check my email and there's a note back from Stella.

I open it eagerly.

My dear Corabelle,

So nice to meet you in Houston and for you to be there for Tina. As you have guessed, it is very common for women to have intense dreams during pregnancy and they often turn pretty dark after one has died.

My best advice to you is for you to learn the parts of a human heart. Look at pictures, see videos of a heart beating. Your mind is putting in the mechanical parts to replace what it doesn't know. It's telling you to learn.

Ask your doctor if you can take a magnesium supplement as well. This will often slow down the whirring of your mind and help your dreams. (Good when you aren't pregnant too.)

Fondly, Stella

I think she's right about this. I don't know why I haven't thought of it. When I picture a human heart, I can see the outside clearly. Red and veined with arteries coming out. But not inside. I can't see that at all.

The search results are immediately helpful. Cutaways show the ventricles and veins. I watch videos of how the blood pulses in and out and even a clip of an open-heart surgery.

It takes some courage to open the next links, but I search "hypoplastic left heart syndrome." This is what Finn had. The doctors had not even tried to fix it, because he was born too early, too weak, and they didn't think he would survive.

There's so much more information now than there was then. The hypoplastic hearts don't look terribly different from healthy ones in the drawings. Narrower arteries, and a left ventricle that is too small. In the images, it seems as if it almost wouldn't matter.

But it does.

When I was researching during the few days Finn was alive, frantically in moments I could get to a computer between time at the NICU, I didn't really look into the likelihood of it happening to another baby. That wasn't even on my mind.

Naturally, it is now.

I type in "genetic cause of HLHS" then shut my eyes. Is this going to help? What could I do about it now? It might make the dreams worse, not better.

A tiny lightning streak of pain shoots through my belly down to my groin. I clap my hand against my stomach. It's gone as quickly as it came, but I snap my laptop shut.

I don't need any more sign than that to stop.

My phone buzzes, but it's clear across the room. I'm not up for moving from my safe place, so I open my laptop again, quickly closing the search results before I can read anything.

My phone messages show up on my messaging app on the computer.

It's Mom.

Gavin's father has heart surgery tomorrow. Very risky. You coming?
What?

I quickly text her back.

What happened?

While I wait for her response, I text Gavin.

What is going on with your father?

My parents have no love lost for the Mays family, who have lived across the back alley since before Gavin and I were born. We never told Mom or Dad outright about Gavin's father, but they knew something at his home wasn't right. They accepted Gavin as one of us.

Well, up until he left during Finn's funeral. That took some work to forgive, for all of us.

I haven't told them about the new baby yet. I don't know why. I'm scared, I guess. And I want to wait for the first sonogram, still two weeks away.

But now this.

Both messages come through at the same time.

From Mom. *He has congestive heart failure and needs a quadruple bypass. I just took a casserole over. I offered to help.*

From Gavin. *The old man's bad karma has finally caught up with him.*

I respond to Gavin first. *When are we leaving?*

He responds: *The day after never.*

Are you sure? It sounds serious.

I'll show up at his funeral and dance on his grave.

Oh, Gavin.

I know. I get it. One of the reasons Gavin and I got so close as children was that Gavin never stayed at home. And when his father forced him to help around the house, I helped too. Mr. Mays wouldn't hit him in front of me.

But when I wasn't around, it was bad. Real bad.

Mom's message is still sitting there, so I answer her.

He won't go.

Not even to let his father make amends?

Is his father planning to?

I don't know. It's so sad. I grieve for Alaina.

My mom and Gavin's mom Alaina became friends after I got pregnant, out of necessity. Gavin leaving town during the funeral hurt their relationship.

Probably Gavin's father has not changed. And Gavin isn't going to give him absolution he hasn't earned.

But I know Gavin is making a mistake. I just know it. Mom thinks Mr. Mays has changed.

I need to make him go. Like lighting the rainbow candle and turning down the adjunct job, I know it's the right thing to do.

8

GAVIN

This is the road trip from hell.

It's a good thing I'm a mechanic, because Corabelle's car is not really up for the challenge of driving from California to New Mexico.

I didn't want to go in the first place, but I'm not one to say no to Corabelle, especially right now, baby and crying jags and all.

So here we are, in the brutal heat of the desert, me trying to coax a failing fuel pump to make it to the next gas station so I can fix it properly.

It's over a hundred degrees, Corabelle's pregnant, and I just want to punch someone in the face.

But instead I lean over the engine, attaching a fuel pressure gauge to the hose.

Zero pressure.

Great.

It's not typical for a fuel pump to go from fine to dead in one trip, so I'm confident I can get it to start up again and run a little longer. We can limp it in. Not the last four hours to Deming. But at least the hour to Tucson. I'll have plenty of car part options there.

"Can you start it up when I say so?" I ask Corabelle.

"Sure." She shifts from where she's leaning against the car, a wet T-shirt wrapped around her neck. Her long skirt whips in the wind. She's been tapping her phone, making sure people know we're out here in case we get stranded. It's seriously the middle of nowhere.

I'm definitely wishing for a rolling creeper as I inch along the dry cracked earth to get under the car. But I have to bang this gas tank and convince the ailing pump to put a little pressure in the fuel line.

"Ready?" I call out.

"Ready!" Corabelle says.

"Fire it up!"

The engine cranks but doesn't turn over. I clang a metal wrench on the tank and tap the motor to the pump to convince the coils to turn.

Corabelle pauses as the car makes noises that probably make her wince.

"Crank it again!" I say. We're close.

She turns it, the starter still hitching. I hear the pump hum for a second, and we should be home free.

The motor catches and the engine fires up. I wait a moment, my back frying against the hot ground, the car rumbling uncomfortably close to my face.

But it stays running. I wiggle out from beneath it.

Corabelle gets out of the driver's seat. "Will it keep going?" Her voice is full of concern. She about panicked when the car sputtered and died in the middle of the highway.

"I'll pick up a new fuel pump in Tucson," I say.

"Isn't Phoenix closer?" She lifts her phone.

"Not much, and it's out of our way."

She walks around to the other side of the car, her long black hair flying in the wind.

I feel like I've eaten dust. I want out of this godforsaken desert.

She turns the air-conditioning vent to her face, eyes closed.

"You okay?" I ask. We were only out there maybe twenty minutes, but it's probably a lot for her right now. When you're already anxious about a pregnancy, stuff like this can tank you.

"I'm okay," she says. Her eyes meet mine and soften.

"We're in this together," I tell her.

She nods.

We take off down the highway again. I pay close attention to my acceleration to make sure the pump is keeping up. I still have a few tricks should it falter again.

It's not an expensive fix, but this car is old and life is just going to get harder when the baby comes. We have to get something reliable for Corabelle.

I'm definitely going to have to drop out of college. We don't even have family nearby to help. Although there's Tina and Jenny. It's just that they both have money, with Tina's husband being a doctor and Jenny's husband signing a record deal. They don't have the problems we do.

Corabelle reaches across the seat, and I take her hand. It's all right that we're not bigwigs. I wouldn't have us any other way.

~*'♥'*~

The stop in Tucson is easy. The fuel pump is only forty bucks there and the manager loans me a couple tools to make it a quick replacement.

The harder thing is actually arriving home.

It's a nine-hour drive normally, and we thought that leaving at eight in the morning would get us to Deming by late afternoon. But the delay means it's after five as we pull into town.

It's still another hour to Las Cruces for the bigger hospital where Dad is, and Corabelle is already looking beat.

"I don't care if I see him before surgery or not," I say.

"There's no point in coming all this way if we don't see him," she says. "Just stop by my house and trade cars. We'll take Mom's the rest of the way."

"This car is fine now," I say.

She flashes me a look and I remember, Corabelle's way. Her hair is stuck to her forehead. I don't think the air conditioner is keeping up with what she needs.

"All right," I say, turning off the highway to the road that will lead to her old house, and mine. I haven't seen any of these places since I left six years ago.

"The old Tiger Mart closed a couple years ago," Corabelle says. "Remember how we used to search for change in the sofa cushions so we could buy candy?"

"Your cushions were always richer than my cushions," I say.

"They were."

It's good to hear her laugh. It helps the curdling feeling I have in my belly. There's lots of good memories with Corabelle as we roll down the streets of our small town. But there's plenty of bad too.

The shed on the lot at the end of the street is gone. I used to hide in it when I needed to escape my dad and Corabelle wasn't home. There's a Walgreens there now.

The houses all seem smaller than I remember, even Corabelle's. We pull up in front of it, the few flowers her mother tries to coax from the arid soil showing their distress.

Mom always planted flowers too. It was something the two mothers would commiserate over, back when they were friends.

The Rothefords come out onto their porch as soon as the first car door closes. Corabelle's father looks the same as always in his baggy dress pants and thick-rimmed glasses. Mrs. Rotheford wears her trademark red lipstick, well put together in a pale green dress, her black hair swept back.

When Corabelle gets out, her mom hurries forward. Mr. Rotheford follows more leisurely, his eyes on me. He's still not one hundred percent happy about my re-entry into Corabelle's life.

They came up last Christmas, and of course we saw plenty of them when Corabelle was in the hospital after her near-drowning incident. I wonder how they'll feel about Corabelle's pregnancy. We're keeping quiet about it this trip. She'll call them in a couple weeks after we have the first sonogram.

They don't know anything about the vasectomy or my reversal. That's the type of thing a couple has to keep to themselves.

"How did the car hold up?" Mr. Rotheford asks, shaking my hand.

"New fuel pump did the trick," I say.

"We thought we'd take your car to the hospital," Corabelle says.

"Of course," Mrs. Rotheford says. She glances at her husband. "We were thinking of coming along too."

"As long as that's okay with Gavin," Mr. Rotheford says. "Tough time for your family."

"Sure," I say. I'm fine with a crowd. If I'm alone with my father, no telling what would go down.

"We have to get going," Corabelle says. "We're so late."

"You sure you don't want to stop and eat something first?" her mom asks. "You look a little peaked." Her gaze slides down Corabelle, and I wonder if she suspects.

Corabelle waves her off. "We had something on the way. Let's go!"

We haul the suitcase inside the house and leave it by the door. Mrs. Rotheford grabs her purse, and I stand there just long enough to get a good strong whiff of their house.

It's amazing how a smell can take you back. For Corabelle's, it's lemon cleaner and a hint of coffee, as her mother drinks it throughout the day. It makes my heart long for simpler times. Before bills, jobs, juggling your hours, and certainly before heartache, worries, and loss.

"Off we go!" Mrs. Rotheford says as she leads us back out on the porch.

We load into the SUV, Corabelle and I sitting close together in the back. It's a different car than I've ever known them to have, but just being there with Corabelle, her parents in the front, gives me that I'm-a-kid-again feel. Someone else is in charge. I relax.

Corabelle leans her head on my shoulder and I kiss her hair. I catch her father watching us in the rearview mirror. He nods a little as he looks away. He's coming around. I don't blame him a bit for any reservations he has about me.

The sun still blazes on the road as we head to Las Cruces. It's a familiar stretch, since as teens, most of us left town every Saturday to find real nightlife. Corabelle remarks on all the changes. Big-box stores. New strip malls. An oversized gas station.

As we approach the hospital, I get more and more leery of what is to come. I have a bonus audience now. I'm not sure if everyone is going to push me forward and expect some heartwarming reunion of father and son.

Because that ain't gonna happen.

Best-case scenario: We all stomp in and my father fails to insult us so badly that I don't walk right back out. We wave. I say, "Good luck," and we go on our way.

That's about as good as I can picture it.

9

CORABELLE

Gavin's death grip on my hand in the car tells me his state of mind. He doesn't want to see his father. He expects it to end badly.

I chatter for a while about the changes along our route, but eventually we all fall silent.

I admit I'm not sure how this will go. My memories of Mr. Mays aren't the best, even though he always acted with self-control around me. I spent a fair number of Saturday mornings at their house, when he would expect Gavin to help him with chores. If I didn't come, things often didn't go well.

One time I thought Mr. Mays would lose it even with me as a witness. We were around twelve, and Gavin was purposefully tweaking his father to anger him more and more. I warned him against this. It was bad enough when he accidentally incited his father to hit him. There was no good in goading him into it.

But Gavin had gotten fed up long before then. And his sister was still quite small, just a toddler. He feared that his father would one day raise a hand to her too. He had it in his head that he could make his father do something bad enough that he'd be put in jail, and the rest of them could live their lives in peace.

That Saturday, they were working on one of the cars as usual, something involving hoses.

Every time Mr. Mays would go around the car, the raised hood blocking his view of the engine, Gavin would pop the hose back off its position.

I sat on the ground with a book of Mad Libs, filling in the nouns and verbs and adjectives, sometimes asking Gavin for one. I remember writing in the margins of the page "This might be bad."

Three times Mr. Mays went to start the car or sort through the toolbox, and three times Gavin unhooked the hose. The first time, his father brushed it off as a mistake. The second time, he gave him a side glance and grumbled about crappy clamps.

But the third time, Gavin couldn't control his smile, and Mr. Mays figured it out.

"Boy," he says. "What the hell you think is funny about a fifteen-minute job taking half the morning?"

His voice had this edge, like someone had roughed it up with sandpaper. It sent a chill through me, and I pulled my knees up to my chest.

Gavin didn't feel like backing down. "Took you long enough to notice," he said.

I winced. What was he doing?

When Mr. Mays lost his patience, I could almost hear it, like a bubble popping. He lifted his right arm, a wrench in his hand.

For a moment, I was shocked silent, picturing that cold metal landing on Gavin's head. I had never felt more scared.

Everything moved in slow motion as Gavin's gaze rose to the raised hand, noticing for himself the tool his father wielded in his fist. This would be it. If he hit Gavin with that and caused enough damage, Gavin would get what he wanted. Police. Arrest. Someone to notice.

But at what cost?

I managed to find my voice and cry, "Don't do it!"

Mr. Mays hesitated, turning as if he had forgotten I was there.

I'm sure I looked pathetic and small, huddling with my book. But it stopped him. He lowered his arm.

"You're useless," he said to Gavin. "Get out of my sight."

Gavin stood his ground, but I wasn't going to let this go on another minute. I scrambled to my feet and grabbed Gavin's arm.

"Come on," I said and started dragging him away.

He resisted, maintaining eye contact with his dad. But I eventually got him to go.

We never told my parents the full extent of what Gavin's father did to him. Maybe they knew. There was evidence. Bruises where bruises shouldn't really be. His reluctance to go home.

Driving down the highway, I wondered — why was that? Why did everyone sit around silent while a man hurt his boy?

"He hit Gavin," I say before my brain can kick in to stop me. "He hit him lots of times."

Gavin lets go of my arm. "Corabelle," he says, a warning note in his voice.

"No," I say. "We're full-grown people. There is no reason to hide this."

I lean forward in my seat. "Mom? Dad? Did you know Mr.

Mays would hurt Gavin? Physically?"

Mom touches her fingertips to her throat but doesn't answer. Dad keeps his gaze out the front windshield, but his grip on the steering wheel gets tight.

"It's not like it was the 1950s or something," I say. "It was 2003 and we should have protected him."

My dad clears his throat. "It's a big thing to accuse someone of, Corabelle. We felt we had a good relationship with Gavin, and if something bad was going on, he would come to us."

Gavin looks out his window, his face averted from me. I don't know what he's feeling, but this has to get out.

"We were just kids," I say. "And scared. I went over there anytime they were together, to try and stop it."

"Oh, Corabelle," Mom says. She turns in her seat. "Why didn't you tell us? It could have put you in danger!"

"He controlled himself when I was around," I say.

"Gavin, talk to us," Mom says.

But Gavin won't acknowledge anyone. He stares out the window, his arms crossed over his chest.

Dad turns on his blinker and pulls over on the side of the highway.

"We sure going to the hospital is a good idea?" he asks.

"That's up to Gavin," Mom says.

I can tell what Gavin is thinking — you drag me here and NOW you decide it's a bad idea? It's obvious from the set of his jaw, the tightness in his fists tucked beneath his arms.

"Gavin," I say. "I think you should see him. I'm the one who brought you here and I knew it all. I just wanted Mom and Dad to understand how deep this goes."

Dad leans his head back on his seat, staring up at the ceiling. "I think," he says, "that everyone deserves the chance to ask for forgiveness before they die. I'm hoping that will be the case for Robert." He turns around to face us.

"Gavin, I feel very complicit in what happened to you," he says. "Maybelle and I certainly saw that you had more injuries than might be expected for a boy, but we didn't ask the right questions. We didn't walk over and ask your parents about it. And we should have. We are sorry."

Gavin relaxes a bit, his arms falling to his thighs. "I wouldn't have admitted it anyway," he says. His voice seems unfazed by the intensity of the discussion, as if we might be talking about somebody else.

Mom reaches through the gap between the seats to touch Gavin's arm. "What would you like, Gavin? We're listening. If you don't think you can handle being near your father even now, we understand."

"We're practically there," he says. "Might as well see it through." His gaze meets mine. "Corabelle is always right on these things."

Dad laughs. "He's got the husband thing down pat."

"Now, Arthur," Mom says.

But the tension has been cut. Dad pulls back out on the highway.

Gavin takes my hand again. We've gotten this out, and now my parents will be on board with however this visit goes. It's what I wanted, for them to understand. For Gavin to be supported even if this meeting doesn't fit their expectations for a father-son reunion.

Now we just have to get there.

10

GAVIN

The hospital looms ahead. Corabelle's father circles it, looking for the guest parking lot.

I'm glad we're not where Finn died. That would have made this trip so much harder. Our baby was life-flighted to El Paso, where a much bigger hospital with a pediatric cardiac unit was housed.

But the Las Cruces medical center is still pretty impressive, all imposing structures and multiple levels.

"You know what room he's in?" Mrs. Mays asks as we get out of the SUV.

"Main building," I say. "Fifth floor."

We wind our way through the rows of cars to the entrance. There's a gift shop just inside, but I'm certainly not going to buy my dad a balloon.

A security guard points out the elevators.

As we rise through the levels, it hits me that I'm about to face my father for the first time since Finn's funeral. He was a big part of why I walked out. That was literally one of the worst days of my life, and the repercussions are only just now getting resolved.

Corabelle squeezes my hand. She looks beautiful, if a little weary. It's been a long day of desert, wind, car repair, and confessions. But she's here. I wonder what would have happened if she wasn't. Mom would have called. I would have refused to come. End of story.

But Corabelle changes every equation, makes my lopsided sums add up.

The elevator stops.

All hospitals smell the same, so I'm momentarily disoriented by memories. Corabelle, after her scare in the ocean. Finn, those tough days living in the NICU. Now my father.

Our somber party of four heads down the corridor. I pause at an intersection, peering at the signs directing us to clusters of rooms. Then I hear "Gavin?"

It's my sister June.

I haven't seen her in six years. She's a young woman already, fourteen and spindly in red shorts and a striped top. But her face is starting to reveal the adult she will become, all dark hair and long lashes.

June rushes for me and almost knocks me backward with her hurtling hug. "Gavin! You're here!"

When my arms go around her, I realize I was right to come here. It's worth a thousand insults from my father to be with her.

My mom appears around the corner. "June, what in the world?" Then she sees me. "Gavin, baby!"

Soon, we're a big clump of huggers. Corabelle gets in the fray. There's crying and hiccups and exclamations.

Mom extricates herself first, smoothing down the front of her floral dress. She looks old fashioned in rose pink, a funny little flower pinned in her graying bun.

And old. The six years have hit her the hardest. Her eyes are deep set in a lined face. Gone are her signature mascara and pink lips.

"Your father is in a room," she says. "They've had to keep him stable since the heart attack so he'd be ready for surgery."

"He's really grouchy," June says. "That's why we were sitting out here."

"Are you staying here in Las Cruces?" Mrs. Rotheford asks. "You must be bone tired."

"We've been sleeping in his room," Mom says.

"Which sucks," June says.

"Watch your language," Mom says.

June rolls her eyes.

Man, my baby sister says "sucks." For the first time since the fuel pump, I manage to crack a smile.

"Why don't you let June come home with us?" Mrs. Mays offers. "If she wants to sleep in her own bed, Gavin can stay with her. Otherwise she is welcome to take our guest room."

"Yes, please, Mom!" June says. "Let me stay with Gavin and Corabelle!"

Mom hesitates, but then rubs her tired eyes. "That might make things easier in the morning. Thank you."

"We're happy to help," Mrs. Rotheford says. She takes Mom into another embrace. "It's been a long time. Too long. Let's catch up." She leads Mom toward the waiting area.

Mr. Rotheford turns to June. "You want to show me the cafeteria? I could use a piece of pie. You think they have some?"

"They do!" she says. "Three kinds! Mom didn't let me have any." She steps closer. "Do we have to ask her?"

Mr. Rotheford leans in close. "I won't tell if you won't." Then to me, "Let your mom know I've taken June with me."

"I will, thanks."

They take off for the elevator, and I look over at Corabelle. "Looks like it's just you and me."

"You want me to go in with you?" she asks.

"Are you kidding? You dragged me here."

She nods. "I'll change how it goes."

"For the better. You always did."

She bites her lip, thinking. "Okay, I'll go in. But if I decide to slip out, you let me go, okay? Trust me?"

I'm not sure I'll stay five seconds longer than she would, but I agree.

We hold hands, dropping by the cluster of chairs to tell Mom where June has gone, and head to Dad's room.

I shouldn't be nervous. He's sick, probably strapped to a bed. And I'm grown, no doubt a million times stronger.

But still, there's that seed there. That little boy who cowered for too long.

We pause outside his door. It's open a few inches.

"Should we knock?" Corabelle asks.

I shrug.

She taps lightly on the door.

His voice booms, unexpected and loud for someone about to

have a quadruple bypass. "Can't a man get any goddamn sleep around here?"

Corabelle and I turn to each other.

"He can't be too close to dying," she whispers.

Figures my dad would be an ass to the end. I push open the door.

He's half lying, half sitting on a bed that's partially raised at the head. He holds a hospital remote in his hand, the coil all caught on his wrist and the side of the bed. He's fighting to get the channel changed.

"No hunting shows whatsoever," he says. "Though I did find some people tracking Bigfoot." He mashes buttons.

It's as if he totally expected me to show and it's no big deal that I've walked in.

"Let me get it untangled," Corabelle says, moving toward him and working on the remote. "Let me hold it."

"Don't hit any buttons," he says. "It was the devil getting the volume right."

She unravels the coil and hands the remote back to him. "There," she says. "How are you feeling?"

"How do you think I'm feeling? I'm all wired up and they're going to crack my chest open tomorrow." He lifts his arms with their tubes and cuffs and IV. "Big waste of time and money. I am fine." His eyes meet mine. "I could walk right the hell out of here."

"I'm sure the doctors know what they're talking about," Corabelle says. "You weren't feeling so great when you collapsed in the garage."

"Ate too much chili, that's all," Dad says. "Everybody's making a big deal out of it."

Corabelle steps back to me. I haven't gotten much past the door.

Dad smirks at us. "You going to say something, son, or just stand there like a damn gargoyle?"

I can't think of a thing to say. Corabelle has already asked how he feels. He's already denounced his need for surgery. I think we're done here.

My weight shifts to step back, but Corabelle holds fast to my arm.

"He came to see you, that's enough," Corabelle says.

"Not sure why if he's not even going to say a blessed 'Hi, how are you.'"

My teeth clench, but I manage to get out, "Hi, Dad, how are you?"

"You got my genes, bud, so you better live clean or you'll end up just like your old man," he says.

"I doubt that," I say.

"Now we're talking," he fires back. "You came to get a couple more potshots at the old geezer before he pops off?"

Corabelle takes that moment to let go of my arm and back up. What is she doing, leaving me already? I'm tempted to follow her, but I say, "Sounds like you could use them."

Dad laughs. "You definitely have a mouth on you now, boy. Get over here so I can see you. They took my damn glasses."

I spot them on a table on the other side of the room and head for it. When I turn around to hand them to Dad, Corabelle is gone.

Great.

"Here," I say, passing them to him.

He takes them and shoves them on his face. "About time.

Now I can actually see the crappy-ass shows." He squints even with them on, peering at the screen. "Damn thing is no bigger than the sixteen-inch I bought your mother when we got married."

"Hospital has all the wrong priorities," I say.

This gets another laugh. "You got funnier too," he says. He watches the show for a moment, then it goes to commercial. "Bah," he says and flips it off. "Sucked anyway."

He tosses the remote on the bed. "I heard you married that girl."

"I did."

"Must really have a number on her, if she took you back after what you did."

He didn't know the half of it. "Meant to be, I guess." I don't really want to talk about Corabelle. That's the fast track to my fist in the jaw of a heart patient.

"She's a good kid."

Huh. I've never heard those words or anything like them come out of his mouth before.

"June seems like she's doing all right," I say.

"Oh, she's a mess. All girly hormones and drama and crying half the time. But she ain't into boys yet. Good thing. I'll geld the sons of bitches if they lay a hand on her."

I have nothing to say to that. My feet are planted near the bed, my hands clasped behind my back. It's awkward, the whole thing.

But I'm doing it.

"You ready for this surgery tomorrow?" I ask. It strikes me that I don't know if my dad gets scared. Maybe all the smoke he's blowing is to cover it.

"Bunch of bullshit if you ask me," he says. But he's already started to slide down on the bed a little, his shoulder drooping. Maybe his big show of strength when we walked in was just that. For show.

"People come through stuff like this just fine," I say. "It's a pretty common thing."

"I wouldn't give two shits if it wasn't for your mother," he says. "But she's weak and couldn't make it on her own."

"She's put up with you for thirty years," I say. "She can't be that weak."

This gets another laugh, lighter this time. "Well, there is that."

He leans his head back and closes his eyes. "Damn nuisance, all this rigmarole."

"You should get some rest," I say. This wasn't too hard. I'm glad Corabelle made me do it. Nobody can say I was a bad son. I showed up when it mattered.

I head for the door.

"Gavin," Dad says.

My body stills. This is it. Will he apologize for all he did? The blows, the welts, the insults, the way he pushed me down until I got too grown, too strong, to let him anymore?

"Yeah?" I turn around. He seems smaller in the bed than when I walked in.

"Why'd you come here?"

I shrug. "Mom asked."

"You don't really give a shit about me, do you?" His eyes bore into me from behind the glasses. I regret giving them to him.

"You're my dad. That makes a certain level of concern automatic."

"Bullshit. You think you're owed something. You came here to see if I was still the same ol' asshole I always was."

"Are you?"

"You think I cuffed you because I was some screwed-up old man. That I wanted to beat kids."

Images roll through my head, his hand coming at me, his belt, a hard shove, a swift kick. Too many times to count.

"You were weak, Gavin. A sniveling little boy. You hung around that girl and were turning into a bona fide pansy. Somebody had to make you tough."

Seriously? He's blaming Corabelle. He's fucking blaming my wife for his BS.

"Shut up," I say. "Don't you bring Corabelle into this or by god I'll rip your heart out by myself."

Now his laugh is back to full power. "See? That's the son I was always looking for you to be." He picks up the remote and turns the TV back on. "I did good," he says. "I did good."

There is no point being here one more minute. I whip around and am out the door before he can say another word.

11

CORABELLE

Gavin is a disaster on the drive back. He won't talk to anyone. Won't even tell *me* what went down in his father's room.

The next morning, when the rest of us get ready to head to the hospital to sit with Gavin's mom, Gavin announces that he and June are spending the day together in Deming.

Mom drops onto an armchair in disbelief. "You're not coming?"

"Nope," Gavin says, brushing donut sugar off his hands. He and June went out early to pick them up. "June is going to show me what's changed in Deming."

"I still need to go," Mom says. "I want to be with Alaina."

"More power to you," Gavin says. "We'll be hiking." He looks at June's tennis shoes. "You got something sturdier than that to wear?"

"At home," she says.

"We'll run by there."

He pauses next to me. "You with us or with them?" he asks.

I have no idea what to do. Gavin is acting like the person in the hospital has nothing to do with him.

"Don't you think your mom would like to see you?" I ask.

He leans down to brush a kiss on my lips. "Her brother will be there. And your mom. I'll take June tomorrow. I hear they don't wake him up for six hours after the six-hour surgery." He glances at his watch. "That's after visiting hours. Tomorrow is better."

Mom reaches out to touch Gavin's arm. "But what if…"

She won't say it.

"He keels over?" Gavin asks. "Then it doesn't matter if I'm there or not. He won't know the difference." He looks at June. "Race you to the back door of our house?"

She lines up as if there's a starting block.

Gavin shouts, "Go!" and they are off, through the living room, past the kitchen, and out the back door. I can see them in the backyard, heading for the gate to the alley.

"Well, I'll be," Mom says. "He seems to be in denial. Did he say what happened last night?"

"Not a word," I say. "But his father was being a real jerk. He probably didn't get any better after I left the room."

"What do you think?" Dad asks. "Should we go without them? Or stay here?"

"I told Alaina I'd be there," Mom says. "I suppose you two could stay."

"I'm going," I say. "His mom might need us if…" I don't say it out loud either.

"I'm happy to chauffeur," Dad says. "Corabelle is here, and

I'm not going to miss out on that."

"Maybe you two could pick up some nice gifts for the family in Las Cruces," Mom says. "It will be a long day in the hospital."

"As long as Corabelle can pick things out, I'm game," Dad says.

Mom sorts through a basket by her feet to pack some knitting supplies in a travel bag. She pulls out a big tuft of fuzzy blue yarn.

My mind stutters for a moment, remembering when she made baby clothes for Finn. The yarn was similar. Finn came early, and she hadn't finished anything but a little hat, which he wore. I wonder what she did with the incomplete booties.

I almost press my hand to my belly, but catch myself. This is no time to announce I'm pregnant. Gavin and I agreed to wait on the sonogram, and I don't want to take away from the seriousness of what is happening in Gavin's family.

We wait around a little while for Gavin and June, but they're obviously already engaged in something fun, so Mom, Dad, and I load up the car.

"It is a little strange to be going up there without either of their kids," Mom says as Dad enters the highway.

"Let them have some fun," Dad says. "Gavin's right, nothing will happen until late afternoon, and it will be evening before anyone can see him."

I sit back in my seat, watching all the same sights go by as the night before. It feels strange to be without Gavin, but I'm glad he'll get some happy time with his sister. Mom seems eager to mend her rift with Gavin's mother.

"Did you ever tell Mr. and Mrs. Mays about the wedding?" I ask Mom.

"I took some pictures over," Mom sighs. "I sure wish Alaina would have brought June. She just wouldn't do it without Robert."

"Gavin didn't want his father there," I say. Neither did I. The two of them together could wreck any occasion.

Mom turns to me. "How bad was it, Corabelle? I can't believe neither one of you came to tell us Robert was hitting Gavin."

"I'm not sure if Gavin left anything out with me. But he often had welts on his back and legs. Sometimes on his face."

"His face!" Mom exclaims. "We would have seen that!"

"He'd stay pretty scarce when that happened," I tell her.

"Did no one notice at school?" she asks.

"I think the teacher asked him about it once, but he didn't tell her," I say.

My father smacks the steering wheel. "We would have taken him in," he says. "Did he hurt June? We will intervene."

"No, he leaves girls alone. It was just about Gavin. I guess he got more frustrated with him." I remember the wrench in the air. So awful.

"Did you ever see it?" Mom asks. Her eyes are wide with worry, probably picturing the things I might have witnessed.

"No, he came close, but he'd behave himself around me. That's why I went over there so often."

Mom's hand flutters to her cheek. "I thought you were helping with the flowers."

"I was. But that was why. I'm not particularly good at gardening."

"My word," she breathes.

"Maybe it IS better if he keels over," Dad says.

"Arthur!" Mom exclaims.

"You think we want a man like that around our grandchildren?" Dad's eyes meet mine in the rearview mirror. "I don't blame Gavin for leaving him out of the wedding."

The word *grandchildren* gets me. I've had myself in check since we arrived, but now tears spring, burning the corners of my eyes. I have to pull it together or Mom will surely guess.

Of course she looks back at me at the worst time. "Corabelle, honey, you okay?" She reaches in her bag and passes me a Kleenex. "You worried about Robert?"

Ha, no. "Just rough times," I say.

"How is grad school going?" Dad asks. "Easier without being a TA?"

I hadn't told them about the adjunct position I turned down, only about finishing my master's without serving as a teaching assistant. Since I'm finishing midyear, I made that my excuse.

"Definitely," I say, wiping my eyes. "I should get my thesis in on time easily."

"Then straight into the doctoral program?" Mom asks. "Are you already admitted?"

"No, applications are due by the end of summer." I won't send one in, of course. I'll have to take at least a year off with the baby. It's a mess, actually. If something bad happens, I won't have a baby or school. I guess I'll go back to Cool Beans for another gap year.

But I can't think that way.

The baby is due in February. I might be able to start my doctorate work the next fall. I don't know. It's overwhelming, all of it. I dab my eyes again.

Mom and Dad exchange a glance, and I know they have

figured out something is up. But it's not time to talk about it.

We're quiet the remainder of the drive. When we get to the hospital, we find they have cleared Gavin's father's room, as they expect him to spend the night in ICU.

"The family will be in the surgical waiting room," the nurse tells us.

We head back to the elevator.

"I haven't seen Ben in ages," Mom says. "I'm glad Alaina's brother can be there, especially if her mother-in-law is coming."

I grimace. I remember Grandma K very well. A sour-faced woman lacking any patience but with more than her share of opinions. Sometimes Gavin and I would cast her as the evil witch in our little plays.

"I wasn't aware I would be sharing a room with Katerina Mays," Dad says. He elbows me. "Let's make a run for it."

"You weren't listening last night," Mom admonishes. "Alaina told us the two of them were coming in."

"I zoned out," Dad says.

"You were playing Plants versus Zombies," Mom says.

"I couldn't let them win!" Dad says. "It's war!"

"Oh, Arthur," Mom says.

I feel better, listening to the amicable teasing that defined my childhood. Instead of the struggling grad student with debt and problems, I'm just somebody's daughter.

The surgical floor is much busier than the regular wards. It's midmorning, and it seems everyone is being wheeled in or out of procedures. Clumps of people stand in the halls, some talking to nurses. We follow the signs to the cardiac ward and spot Gavin's mom in the chairs of a large waiting area. Grandma K is next to her.

"There she is," Dad says through clenched teeth.

Gavin's grandmother looks exactly the same as the last time I saw her, at Finn's funeral. Stout, dressed in a vivid green muumuu, her silvery hair spun into a wispy puff, her pale scalp showing through.

She holds a red purse in her lap, clamped with both hands. She stares straight ahead. I'm not sure if she's worried about her son, or this is just her usual surly self.

Gavin's mother stands when she sees us. "Maybelle, Arthur, so good of you to return." She kisses Mom's cheek. "And Corabelle." She looks behind us. "Where is Gavin? And June?"

"He didn't message you?" Mom asks, casting a worried glance my way. "He and June are back in Deming. He didn't see a reason to put June through a long day of waiting up here. They'll come when there is news."

"Oh," she says. "I guess that is good for June." She glances back at Grandma K. "Ben hasn't made it yet. He's driving down from Phoenix."

She sits down, and Mom takes a seat beside her. No one speaks to Grandma K. Dad and I glance at each other. There's only one seat by Mom. The other is on the other side, next to Grandma K.

Dad leans in. "Arm wrestle you for it."

I laugh. "We can go in the row behind."

"You were always the smart one," he says.

We settle in behind the two mothers. Grandma K still hasn't glanced our way. I lean close. "Hello, Grandma K," I say.

She grunts, her eyes still forward.

Gavin's mom glances back at me and gives the tiniest shrug.

78

"I'm so glad I could be here," Mom says. "I assume Robert has already gone back?"

"He's in prep," Mrs. Mays says. "Surgery is supposed to begin at nine."

That's in ten minutes. I imagine surly Mr. Mays back there in his hospital gown, all mean eyes and patchy whiskers, insulting everybody right to the end. They'll probably enjoy putting the mask on him and watching him go under.

Stores won't open until ten. I settle in by Dad and plan to just wait. This is what family does.

Even when the one you're sitting here for is an obstinate, awful, horrible man.

Maybe this brush with mortality will be the thing that changes him.

12

GAVIN

My little sister is fun.

We've decided on Cooke's Peak. She didn't have anything resembling hiking boots, but she's only one size smaller than our mother. And Mom had an ancient pair, probably from her youth, but in decent shape. With two pairs of socks, they work.

So we're off.

I've loaded a string bag with water and lunch. We have hats shading our faces, and I was the responsible brother, making June put on sunscreen.

It's weird, seeing her as a real person and not a little girl. She was only eight when I left. The last thing I remember was how she clung to Corabelle's mom, asking if she was still an aunt now that Finn was dead.

She looks nothing like that now, lanky in jeans and a pink T-shirt with a kitten on it. Her long brown hair is in a ponytail.

"Doing all right?" I ask as the trail moves from dirt to rock.

"Totally. This is fun!" She picks her way across a bigger cluster and we settle onto dirt again. "Mom and Dad never take me anywhere."

"What about your friends?" I won't admit it, but I worry about her, isolated in that house with my surly father and a mother who believes in obeying her husband.

"They're okay, but it's more about texting and hanging out at home. They're not very outdoorsy."

I'm glad to hear she has other places to go. "You have a phone already?"

"Duh! I'm fourteen!" Her eyes roll.

It makes me laugh. "I didn't have a phone at fourteen," I say.

"You didn't need one. You lived at Corabelle's and never talked to anybody else."

She pushes ahead of me on the narrow trail. Around us, scrub brush and rocks start their rise toward the summit. Beyond that, dry dead grasses lie listlessly against the earth.

We can make it about two-thirds of the way before we'll get to the hard scrabble. But the part we're tackling is a fine hike anyway, a good-enough challenge to make you feel like you're really doing something.

We trudge along in silence a while, hearing little but the sound of the ground crunching beneath our feet. As the incline begins and the rocks get larger, something you have to hold on to and climb, we see a couple other hikers ahead. They're more experienced, though, and take off for a tall face you have to climb with ropes. We head the other direction for rocks you can pick your way through without equipment.

After about an hour, I ask her, "How far you want to climb?"

"I can keep going."

"Remember we have to go back down."

She looks behind us. "Way easier going down than up!"

True, although it can be tricky on the rocks.

We keep going.

Cooke's Peak is six miles each way, and I figure we've covered maybe two of them. But it's cathartic, the decisions simple, one path or the other, this rock or that. It's like a puzzle laid out by nature, asking us to unlock its secrets and see the magic of the whole view once it's put together.

After a second hour, we stop and eat. It's hot now, the sun beating down.

"Glad you got these hats," June says, gulping down her PB&J.

"Yeah, it's brutal." I'm glad Corabelle didn't come. She's already anxious enough about the pregnancy. This would definitely be too much.

When we've put everything away, I ask, "Up or head back?"

She turns her face to the sun. "Let's keep going."

I point out the upper face. "If we head that way, we might be able to get to the top of the short side. It's not the highest peak, but it's something."

"A top is a top," she says.

We move forward, the terrain growing increasingly difficult. We should've worn gloves. My palms and fingertips get rough and sore. But June doesn't complain.

Up and up we scale the side. Sometimes I have to jump on a large rock and turn to pull June up. We don't talk about anything more than the immediate situation — *left or right? Is that rock too big?*

Watch out for that hole.

I learn more about her than if I had talked to her at home. She's tough. She's smart. She analyzes situations well. She plans ahead. And most of all, she sticks with something even when it's hard.

The wind starts rushing at us. The air feels different.

"We're getting close!" I say.

And we are. It's a fight to make it up the last part, as scrub brush and crumbling rocks threaten most every path. But then we clamor over a particularly tricky spot and there it is.

The top.

Even my meager hair gets tossed every direction. June's ponytail whips away from her head.

It's perfectly warm and perfectly cool, all at the same time. It feels as though we're in the vortex of a storm, the air spinning as if it doesn't know which way to blow.

"Wow," June says. It's hard to come up with words to describe how it feels.

The desert stretches out far beyond the foothills. The roads are tiny ribbons eventually disappearing into the dust.

We sit down, and once again, we don't need to talk about anything at all. Everything we might want to say is all laid out in front of us. How hard a road we've traveled. How terrible a place we just left behind, Dad in the hospital and finding it hard to care one way or the other.

But the flip side is just as clear. The unbroken beauty of the sky. The wildness of the wind, unchanneled and blowing free.

For this moment, we see exactly how beautiful it can be to push through the hardship and reach the top.

13

CORABELLE

Dad and I sit in the waiting room far longer than we intend. Mom knits and speaks quietly to Gavin's mom. Grandma K keeps her glowering vigil.

I'm not feeling super well, so I'm staying put.

In the two weeks since the positive pregnancy test, I have felt perfectly fine. Tina says she's not as sick as the first time, so I assumed I was just seasoned in this pregnancy thing and morning sickness wouldn't be as debilitating as it got with Finn.

Right now, I'm realizing I was wrong.

I sincerely regret eating one of the donuts Gavin and June brought this morning.

The milk, even more.

I take deep calming breaths, sure the tummy upset will remain an internal discomfort and not make itself known to the spectators in the waiting room.

I am wrong again.

The eruption is so sudden and unexpected that I don't even have time to aim. I turn my head away from my father, managing to throw up down the back of the chair in front of me.

Grandma K's chair.

Oh, God.

"I'm so sorry," I say, looking around, trying to find anything I can to clean it up.

I lift my skirt, but my mother says, "Don't soil your dress, Corabelle. I'll get some paper towels from the bathroom."

The trouble is, more is coming.

I push past my dad and race for the door ahead of Mom. I don't know where the bathroom is exactly, but I'd rather upchuck in the hall than on anyone else in the room.

My stomach roils. Why did I eat that donut? Why is this hitting me now?

"To the left," Mom says behind me, and I turn that way, relieved to see the little male/female symbol above a door to indicate a family bathroom.

I'm barely inside before it comes again. I spot the sink first, and aim for that.

Pink sprinkles. Gross.

I flash my hand across the sensor under the faucet to wash the evidence away. Of course the drain is too fine and it won't go down.

This is horrible.

"Stay right here," Mom says. "I'm going to run some wet paper towels to Katerina and I'll be right back."

She douses a handful under the spray and takes off.

I pull a few paper towels out myself and try to clean the sink. My stomach heaves again, but now it's empty, so nothing comes out.

Enough already, baby. We're done here.

Mom returns. "Let me get that," she says. She glances around. "There's no place to sit in here."

I lean on the cold counter beside the sink. "I'll be all right."

"You nervous about Robert?" she asks.

"That and I should have skipped the donut."

She nods. "I knew better than to eat one on a day like this."

Relief washes over me that she's accepting my explanation. But I am still in misery. And too embarrassed to go back in where Grandma K is trying to clean herself up. God. Her son is having heart surgery and her granddaughter-in-law would have to puke on her.

I want to crawl in a hole.

"Maybe Dad should take you home," she says.

"But it's an hour away," I say. "And you're here."

"I'll be fine. He can come for me later, or I can stay here with Alaina." She presses her mouth in a tight line, and I know she's realized this means she won't get to spend this time with me. We're only here for a few days. We can't afford for Gavin to take off more than that. Plus my summer classes.

My stomach heaves again, and I cough over the sink.

Mom frowns. "You'd think you'd feel better once the food was out."

I have to pull myself together. I tug another paper towel out, wet it, and place it against my head. "No telling," I say.

"We should stay in here until it passes."

"Probably." Except it might not pass for a while. I remember marathon morning sickness with Finn, lying on the bed with my head hanging off, trash can directly below.

"Can you get to the car?" she asks.

I nod.

"Let me get your father. We'll get you down."

"Okay."

She heads out again.

God. This is too much. Maybe I should confess. My stomach sucks in, twisting, heaving. I cough into the sink, futilely. Come on, baby, please. Stop.

I remember mornings with Finn when Gavin would bring me crackers right as I woke up. Eating something simple could ward off the worst of it. I'd forgotten those times. How sick I could get.

I had no idea at the time that those were the best days.

These might be the best days now.

I stand up, twisting my hair in a knot and tucking it in on itself. I can pull myself together. Mind over stomach.

Six or seven more paper towels would make a decent stash for the car. I fold them together and stick them in my purse. Then I wet a couple more and tuck them inside the collar of my shirt to keep my neck cool. That helps, I remember doing it before.

I rinse out my mouth a few times and stand up straight.

Corabelle Rotheford Mays, you are going to walk out of here, get in the car, and be absolutely fine until you get home.

I nod at myself and open the bathroom door.

Mom and Dad are already coming down the hall, looking serious.

"How are you feeling, Tinker Bell?" Dad asks.

"Better now."

"You ready for me to take you home?"

"Yes. Is Grandma K all right?"

Dad smirks. "She'll survive. Mom's going to drive her to her hotel to change while Alaina stays."

"I'm going above and beyond on this one," Mom says. "But Alaina's brother will be here any minute, so she won't be alone for long."

We head down the hall. Each step is torture, a full-blown headache blooming behind my eyes. Mom hugs us and turns into the waiting room. I don't look inside to see what havoc I've wrought. Dad and I continue on to the elevator.

Only when we're back in the car do I relax a little. I spread out some of the paper towels just in case.

Dad pulls out of the parking lot. "Not used to donuts in the morning?" he asks, but I can tell that is not the question. He suspects.

"It was a terrible idea," I say.

"It was a delicious idea," he counters.

The pause after this is long, but he doesn't press.

I'm torn. I've gotten away with it this morning. But if I'm this sick again tomorrow, or even later today, they will figure it out.

I don't know why I'm so afraid to tell them. I should be celebrating this little life, not hiding it.

But it's a common feeling. Women who get pregnant again after losing a baby often don't tell anybody the news until they have to.

Today it's perfectly clear to me why. When only we know about the baby, it's so much simpler. There are no tragic phone calls to make, no Facebook statuses to write. No sad faces looking at you. No terrible clichés repeated.

It's just you. You and your pain, your emptiness, your loss.

For some reason it feels like that will be easier.

But I have a feeling that this isn't true at all.

It's all hard. All horrible.

There is no good answer for any of this. Instead of the warm joy of anticipation, I live with the cold breath of fear.

14

GAVIN

Mom calls when June and I are most of the way down the mountain, tiredly clomping along the flatter part of the trail.

I figure it's right about the time the surgery is done. I don't figure he survived the whole six hours only to die at the end. So he's probably okay.

"Hey, Mom," I say.

June halts, her eyes wide. I should have said something to her before I answered.

"I'm going to put you on speaker with me and June," I add.

We sit on a rough boulder, me holding the phone between us.

"Your father is out of surgery," Mom says. "They said it all went fine. Took three arteries out of his leg and two out of his arm."

"Gross," June says.

I nod my agreement.

"That's what they have to do," Mom says. "He's in ICU, of course, so I haven't seen him. They will let him sleep off the anesthesia, so he won't wake until later tonight."

"How you holding up?" I ask.

"I'm fine. Maybelle is here. Corabelle and her father left after she threw up all over Grandma K."

June lets out a snort, then claps her hand over her mouth.

Uh-oh. Morning sickness must have hit. "Is Corabelle okay?" I ask.

"Maybelle said it was probably nerves."

I know better. "Okay. I'll check on her."

"They've been home a long time by now. You went on a hike, they said?"

"Yeah," I tell her. "Cooke's Peak."

"That's a big hike!" she says. "Is June all right?"

"I'm fine, Mom," June says. "We made it to the top!"

"Oh my," Mom says. "I assume I won't see you tonight?"

"You spending the night there?" I ask.

"I have a hotel room," she says. "With my brother Ben. He's here. I can't sleep in the ICU like I did his room."

Right. "Well, fill us in tomorrow and maybe I'll take June up there," I tell her.

My sister whacks my arm. "I'm not going if you're not."

"You will both come up here," Mom says. "You're his family."

"Okay, Mom," I say, giving my sister some hard-core side eye.

"And let me know how Corabelle is," Mom says. "She looked positively green."

"Will do."

I end the call. June hops off the rock.

Corabelle hasn't messaged me today at all, and nobody has told me she was sick. I remember the tough time she had with Finn the first few months and worry that this is the beginning of that again. It will be hard to hide the pregnancy from her parents if it keeps up on this trip.

I want to shoot her a message, but June keeps going, so I have to hurry to catch up. We'll talk when I get back, I guess. She would have called me if anything big was happening. The fact that her mother stayed with mine means it was minor.

"I wish I could have seen Corabelle barf all over Grandma K," June says. "That would have been awesome."

"She's probably mad as hell," I say.

"She deserves it," June says. "You've gotten to miss all the horrible Christmases with her yelling at everybody all day."

"I remember those." Guilt washes over me that I wasn't there to make those days better for June. "How has Dad been since I left?"

"I dunno. Angry and brooding as ever. He has a hard time keeping anybody working with him. They quit after a few months."

Dad does landscape work. He usually has some sort of assistant, as some of the jobs require a lot of lifting and grunt work. I'd helped him most summers growing up.

Sounds like they are getting the brunt of the anger he used to save for me.

"Is he all right around you and Mom?" I ask her this whenever we talk on the phone, but she always says he's fine. Face to face, though, I can judge her expression when she answers.

"He's a jerk, like he's always been, and I can't stand it when he yells at Mom." She jumps over a boulder on the path. Our conversation has gotten her energy up again. "I know I'm supposed to love him because he's my dad. But I don't know if I do. Does that make me a bad person?"

"No, no," I say. "It makes you a sane person. He hasn't earned it."

"I don't know why Mom stays with him."

"I had the same questions when I got to be your age. Still don't have the answer."

"Did she get knocked up or something? I always thought they were married a couple years before you came along."

"They were. Maybe he was different back then."

We stamp along. June is slowing down again.

This much alone time with my sister is a rare opportunity. I want to make absolutely sure Dad isn't getting physical with her.

"June, has Dad ever hit you?"

"He spanked me once. Not long after you left. It made me laugh for some reason. He didn't do it again."

"You laughed?"

She cracks a smile. "I know, weird, right? He just looked so silly, trying to catch me and swat my butt. He's slow, you know."

"But he's still mean."

"He's never anything but mean."

We reach the trailhead and walk along the road to Corabelle's car.

"Gavin?" June says, peering at me through the glare.

"Yeah?"

"Are you and Corabelle going to have another baby?"

At first I think she's asking if Corabelle is pregnant, but then I realize it's a general question.

"Sure," I say.

"I sure would like to be an aunt," June says.

"You'll be a good one."

"I want to be an aunt like Uncle Ben is an uncle. Funny and silly."

"He's a great example."

June gets serious. "You think I'll be a good parent? I don't think we had good examples for that."

Her question strikes right at my heart. I reach out and tweak her ponytail. "They just taught us what not to do. Now we'll be perfect at it."

She laughs and ducks away from me. "No, I will be perfect. You'll just be my stinky big brother!"

June takes off running for the car, and despite my own exhaustion, I speed after her. I miss her. Maybe we can take her back with us for a while. It's summer.

Except Corabelle is in school. And I work. Damn.

I'll just have to take this moment and hold on.

15

CORABELLE

By the time Gavin and June are back, I'm feeling well enough to fake it. Dad has ordered pizza.

The four of us sit in the sunroom looking out on the backyard. Mom's planted more flowers there and coaxed them into blooming even in the desert. That's what she does.

June is animated and lively, talking about her hike. I'm glad Gavin did this with her. It's clearly a very special memory for her already.

The sun starts to set. Dad stacks the plates.

"Coming up on seven," he says. "Seems like we should be hearing about your dad waking up soon."

Gavin and June get all still. I don't know what that means for either of them. Probably Gavin cares more than he wants to admit. June must be terrified.

"You want to go up there?" Gavin asks his sister.

"Maybe," she says. "Mom probably wants us."

"Let's go." He stands up and pulls the keys to our car out of his pocket.

"Take mine," Dad says. "Keys are in the kitchen."

"You coming?" Gavin asks me.

"You can puke on Grandma K again," June says with a giggle. "I totally want to see that."

"I'm not sure I want to see her again just yet," I say. Which is true. I also don't want to have my stomach vibrate in a car for an hour after eating pizza, not that I ate much. Just enough to escape notice.

Gavin leans over and kisses my hair. "We'll be back tonight." To my dad he says, "We'll bring Mrs. Rotheford back."

"Sounds good," Dad says. "Let us know how your father is doing."

"Will do."

The two of them head out the front door. In the quiet of the early evening, I can hear the car start up.

I take a stack of cups and follow Dad to the kitchen. It's bright and colorful, like only happy things can happen here. Mom has changed out the curtains since I lived here, but the orange and white stripes have the same sunshiny feel as the yellow ones she had before.

Dad opens the dishwasher and starts loading plates in. "I'm thinking of trading cars with you," he says. "That battle-ax of yours isn't safe."

I hand him a cup. "You don't have to do that, Dad. We're getting by."

"Grad school is tough enough," he says. "I'll trade your old one in. Your mom's been angling for a new one anyway."

"I'll talk to Gavin about it." He can be proud, even though an SUV would be a lot more convenient with the baby.

If the baby comes.

"So when do you plan to tell your mom and me about the baby?" he asks, sticking a plate on the bottom rack as if this is any old question.

My breath sucks in. "What?"

"Your mom won't ask about it. She thinks if you're not telling us, you have your reasons. But she's not here. So I'm asking."

I should have known they would figure it out.

"When did you know?"

"The minute Gavin walked you in like you were made of glass. He acted just the same with Finn."

Hearing someone else say his name out loud makes my heart clench.

Finn.

"And then I got sick this morning," I say.

"And pizza is usually your favorite," he adds. "You only ate a few bites to throw me off."

Obviously that hadn't worked.

I sit on a stool by the bar. "I'm due in February," I say. "I just found out two weeks ago."

"Seen the doctor yet?" He sticks the last plate in the rack and dries his hands.

I shake my head. "I'm scheduled for nine weeks, but I can come in earlier if I want."

"They know what happened last time?"

"They do. We can't do a sonogram to check this one's heart

until I'm at least sixteen weeks along."

"Whew. That's a long time."

"I know."

"How are you and Gavin for health insurance? A sick baby is a huge expense." He leans against the counter, his face etched with concern.

"Gavin's garage doesn't have benefits, but we bought an independent policy a few months back." I don't mention that we did this before the reversal surgery, in case something went wrong. Insurance wouldn't cover the reversal, but complications would be part of the plan.

"Does it cover maternity?"

"Yes. We made sure."

"So you planned this? Even with grad school?" His question carries a note of disapproval.

"I know. We should have prevented. We just didn't. My two best friends have started families." I stop. I can't explain how I really felt. Like I needed to try again. That I felt like a failure and I wanted to fix this hole, if it could ever be mended.

"Do you need help? I can send your mother up there."

"No, no," I say. "I'm fine. I have a scholarship right now and I'm not having to work beyond school and my thesis. It's actually the easiest load I've had in a while."

"Gavin still on course to graduate?"

"Eventually. He's taking off this summer, of course, and putting in extra hours. I'll try to make sure he goes back in the fall."

"That degree is important if he wants to do more than be a mechanic. That's honest work, to be certain, but it's a waste of all those years of study."

"I know."

Dad walks over and curls his arm around my neck. "Don't feel like you have to hide something like this from us, Tinker Bell. We're here to support you."

My eyes prick with tears. "I know, Dad. It's just so hard and scary. I don't want to feel like I caused other people sadness and fear too."

"But we want the chance to help. It's worth risking those hard feelings."

I nod against his chest. He smells like Woolite and desert air. Like my childhood. Like home.

I'm glad we're here.

"Let's head back to the sunroom," he says. "It's always been the good place in the house."

"It has," I say. We walk that way, to the wicker furniture with overstuffed cushions, Mom's indoor plants, and the huge glass windows. I want to ask him something hard, and it's better to do it there.

When we're settled again, I gather my courage, then ask it. "Dad, did the doctors ever figure out why Mom lost those four babies?"

His eyebrows lift above the rim of his glasses. "Well, that's been a lot of years ago. But when Finn was diagnosed, we went over all that paperwork again. Mom even called her old ob/gyn's office. Dr. Jenner is long retired, but the clinic is still around."

"What did they say?"

"In those days, they didn't test like they do now. But it seems like the problem was with the shape of your mother's womb. Nowadays they do some surgery to correct it, I believe. But then you just had to hope one of the babies would make it through. Like you."

"So no heart problems in the babies?"

"Not that we knew about. One of the babies was…" he hesitates, then coughs into his hand. My eyes spring with tears again. Faking a cough is how he's always covered his emotions.

He begins again. "One of them was fully formed. A boy. Stillborn. But yea big." He holds his hands about a foot apart. "Looked perfect." He brushes his graying hair back even though it's nowhere near his face.

"They did an autopsy. But nothing wrong. Not a thing. Just died inside her. They think he didn't get enough blood supply. He was small for what he should have been."

"Did you give him a name?"

Dad shakes his head. "No, that wasn't really done then. We only saw him a minute or two before they whisked him off. They said the more we held him, the worse we'd feel. Didn't get any pictures or anything." He taps his temples. "He's just up here."

"That's terrible," I cry. The pictures I have of Finn are the most important things I own. They are what got me through.

"I understand things are different now. They let you hold on to them. Do special photo shoots and all. That's good." He nods vigorously and clears his throat.

"I don't have a problem inside," I say. "Nobody has said anything if I do."

"You're probably all right then," he says. "And this baby should be too."

A few hot tears track down my face for all my parents lost before me. So much pain in the world. It is hard to bear.

We sit in the sunroom as the day comes to a close. The yellow light fades across the alley, disappearing over Gavin's house just beyond the fence. I hope he and June are doing all right, and that whatever happens with his father is something everyone can handle.

Life is precious and fleeting. Seven days for Finn. Forty-seven years so far for Mr. Mays. We have to hold on to every moment and make them count.

16

GAVIN

The hospital seems quieter than last night. Maybe it's because we're walking to ICU rather than a normal patient hall.

Everyone inside this waiting room is somber. Makes sense, I guess. Cases here are more serious. People probably die on this ward every day. Maybe several times a day.

I shouldn't think like that.

Mom is in the back corner, talking quietly with Uncle Ben. She looks like a widow already, in a black sweater and skirt. Ben listens carefully, nodding at the right moments. He's grizzly, with a big beard that obscures much of his face. That's new.

"Where's Grandma K?" June whispers.

"Heck if I know," I say. "You want me to go find her so you can give her a big ol' hug?"

June stabs my side with her elbow. "Hush."

Only six or seven other people are scattered through the

room. In the opposite back corner, two women weep softly in a huddle. My stomach flips. I wonder what they're going through.

I snuck into an ICU in California once to see Corabelle. The actual ward, not the waiting room. The beds had all been lined up along the wall, monitors beeping at random intervals.

I got caught, but the nurse had mercy and let me stay. Corabelle had pneumonia, a bad case. I was beside myself, thinking I had found her after four years only to lose her again.

This time is nothing like that. I try to find any concern for my father at all, and come up with nothing. If he's dead, he can't insult Corabelle. Blaming her for the way he treated me was ridiculous. Anger burns in my heart a second time, just thinking about it.

"June," Mom says, holding out her arms.

June walks over reluctantly and allows Mom to wrap her up in a hug.

"Uncle Ben is here!" Mom says.

Ben must not have been around much in the last six years, because June gets shy when she turns to him. He holds out a hand and she shakes it awkwardly.

I guess I better get over there too.

"Gavin," Uncle Ben says, standing to clap my back as we shake. "You're not the teenage pipsqueak I saw last."

"You look like you've filled out a bit yourself," I say.

Ben spreads his hands across his belly. "Looking to apply for some Santa positions soon," he jokes. "Just waiting on this hair to go gray."

"Oh, you've got years on that," Mom says. "Dad didn't go gray until he was sixty."

And died not long after, I recall. His favorite expression was "die young and leave a good-lookin' corpse." He hadn't died all that young, but certainly before any of us was ready.

Grandpa Jack hadn't cared one whit for my father and told Mom so. I heard them argue a time or two that she should leave him. But Mom always stuck by her husband. That's what she always did best.

Sometimes I imagine Grandpa Jack and Finn are in some otherworldly play land, whooping it up together. Life sure was all right when he was around, giving me geodes and making sure I was learning stuff. He did hard labor on road construction sites, and it broke him down over time. His son Ben followed in his footsteps. He wanted something different for me.

Maybe I needed to get that degree done after all.

I sit by Ben, and June settles in next to Mom.

"Any news?" I ask.

"They update us every couple hours," Mom says. "Everything looks good, so they're going to let him wake up on his own. He's ornery enough that he'll make us wait all night."

"You want to get some dinner or some sleep?" I ask. "I can hang out up here."

"Ben and I had dinner," Mom says. "We're going to give it until midnight then break until morning."

That's about four hours away. "They let you stay here all night?"

"Sure," Mom says. "New people come in fairly regular. I think they bring them up here from the ER if they aren't stable enough for a regular room."

"Some sad cases in here," Uncle Ben says. His eyes dart to the weeping women. "Car accident. Teen daughter killed. Husband here after emergency surgery."

My gaze skitters over them again.

I wonder what we look like to the others. Indifferent son. Unaffected daughter.

It was different with baby Finn. We were in the NICU and everyone's situations were obvious. Each row was a different level of care. Finn was in the most fragile row.

Many of the babies on his row didn't go home.

Here, you don't see the same people day in and day out. Everyone moves all over.

A nurse comes in, nondescript in blue scrubs and black hair tied up tight. The room looks up expectantly, wondering who is getting news.

She heads toward us. "You all are for Robert Mays, right?"

"We are," Mom says.

"He's awake. Only two can come back at a time, for five minutes only," she says. She looks at June. "How old is she?"

"How old does she need to be?" Uncle Ben asks.

Mom elbows him. "She's fourteen. His daughter."

"That will be all right," the nurse says. "Who is first?"

Mom stands. "June? Gavin?"

My sister and I look at each other. Neither of us makes a move.

"I'll go," June says with a sigh.

They follow the nurse out of the room.

Uncle Ben leans his head against the wall. "Been a long day in these chairs," he says.

"I bet."

"I heard you drove up last night."

"Yeah. Corabelle made me come." I lean over and brace my elbows on my knees. My boots are covered in dust from the hike.

"I didn't figure you'd do it. You've been scarce a while."

I shrug. "She's got my number."

This gets a laugh. "I hear ya on that. Not much Phoebe asks for that I don't do."

Aunt Phoebe. I hadn't thought about her in a long time. She didn't always come up with Uncle Ben. They have an autistic son and travel is difficult.

"How is she? And James?"

"Percolating along. James ages out of public school next year, so we'll have to figure out what's next."

"Is he doing okay?"

"He's starting to say a few words." Uncle Ben rubs his eyes. "He understands everything we say. Sometimes he'll do what we ask, sometimes not. He just can't say anything back. Not sure he ever will."

My eyes drop back to my feet. So many ways parenting can be hard.

"You and Corabelle going to try and have another kid?" he asks.

Great. What to say to that?

"We are," I say. That's true either way you look at it.

Another nurse comes in and heads to the corner with the weeping women. Their faces lift, fear layered over the grief.

The woman says something in hushed tones and the two of them gather their things. Has the husband been moved to a regular room and will recover? Or are they being taken to one of those awful grieving rooms to be told he has not made it?

I'll never know. They will walk out and their story will remain unfinished to me.

"Tough place to be," Uncle Ben says. "I'm going to go down for some coffee. Want any?"

I shake my head. "I'm good."

He stands up and heads for the door.

For a crazy moment I consider following the women, see where they go. I want to know someone else's ending.

But Uncle Ben is only gone a moment when Mom and June return.

"You're next," June says. "He's really out of it. He barely knew who I was." She plunks back down on a chair.

"We'll wait for you to come back, then you can take June home with you," Mom says. "Just go past that desk and around to the first door on the right. He's in the fourth bed."

"All right." I head through the chairs. Figures I would be heading back there alone. But if he's like June says, it won't matter. I can say "good-bye and get better," and my duty here is done.

The woman at the desk nods to me as I pass. Then there's a narrow hall and a couple doors. I take the first one.

The ward is semi-dark, lights flashing from machines set at intervals. I count the beds, one, two, three, four, and I see him. He's still flat on his back, arms stretched out on the bed. A nurse sits beside him.

She nods at me. "He's still going in and out a bit. It will probably be tomorrow before he really comes around."

I stand next to the bed. Dad has a million wires coming from him and an oxygen tube in his nose. Next to him, a machine lights up with his pulse. Quadruple bypass. And yet, the heart keeps on beating, like nothing's happened at all.

I wonder if this is my future, or if his way of living got him here. Something to ask a doctor about sometime, I guess.

The nurse touches his arm. "Robert, your son is here."

His eyes flutter at that, then open. He's groggy, looking around like he's trying to place himself. Then his gaze falls on me.

I can't be too clear, not without his glasses.

"Hey," I say. "Just stopping by. I'm about to take June back."

He nods at me, and I think maybe he's glad I came, at least to be there for my mother and sister. And he's right. Putting up with him is worth it if I can have more time like the hike I had with June.

He tries to lift an arm, realizes it's tethered, and drops it down again. Then his mouth opens, but nothing comes out.

"It's all right, Robert," the nurse says. "Your throat will be a little dry for a while from the anesthesia tube." She lifts a cup with a straw. "Take a little sip."

He does so, and gives a weak cough. His heart monitor jumps, and I'm startled, picturing the new veins breaking away, spewing blood through his chest.

The nurse pats his shoulder. "That's good," she says. "Settle back." She sets the cup down. "He seems fragile, but we'll have him up and walking by morning, most likely."

That seems wild. They cracked open his chest and stopped his heart. But tomorrow he'll be out of bed.

He's more awake now, and the eyes that fix on me are harder again. "Boy," he says.

I know that tone. One more insult for the road.

"Yeah?" I ask.

"Stop staring at me like I'm gonna die," he rasps. "You look like a scared rabbit."

And with that, I've officially had enough.

"See ya later," I say. "Be nice to Mom and June or I'll rip those new veins out myself."

The nurse drops her jaw in shock as I turn on my heel and walk straight out.

17

CORABELLE

I honestly don't know any details about how Gavin's father's recovery goes after we leave town, as Gavin won't talk about him. I assume he's okay since I talk to my own mom every other day now that she knows I'm pregnant. She says he came home after a few days. She was in her backyard and heard him cussing in his.

I'm sad there was no change to their relationship. Maybe that was too much to hope for.

Tina gets married to her doctor. Her wedding is simple, our star-spangled arch carried out to a cliff overlooking the ocean. It's a special place for her and Dr. Darion. She lets her baby Peanut's ashes go at the end of the ceremony and it's all I can do not to break down over it.

I'm not as able to let go as she is.

The day of the first sonogram arrives, and Gavin takes off work to go with me. I'm not particularly nervous about this one. I expect everything to go fine for a while.

Dr. Jamison comes in, dressed in surgical scrubs. "Sorry for the garb, expecting a delivery next door today." The medical building is adjacent to the hospital where Jenny had her baby girl.

It was also where I was taken after nearly drowning in the ocean.

So much has happened here.

The doctor shakes hands with me and Gavin. "I hear we've got a baby coming!" he says. His dark hair and bright eyes help me feel calm. I can see why Jenny likes him.

"We met once before," I say. "When my friend Jenny had her baby early. She went into labor during a concert. I was with her."

"Oh, yes! Jenny is a lively one," he says. "How is her little girl doing?"

"Great," I say. "She's crawling and everything."

Dr. Jamison flips through my chart. He's still old-school with a manila folder and printed pages attached with big gold fasteners.

"I see here you've had a baby once before," he says. "Premature delivery. Congenital heart condition."

I nod, my throat thick. "They didn't operate. He died at seven days old."

"I'm so sorry." His eyebrows knit together, and I can see he really means it.

I manage to keep my voice even as I say, "I read we won't be able to check this baby's heart until sixteen weeks."

"It won't be conclusive until then, and if there is a minor defect, maybe not even then," he says. "A lot of us walk around with minor heart problems that are never detected in our lifetime."

"Finn's wasn't minor."

"We can do a genetic study if you like," he says. "We can pull an amnio, do the karyotype on you two as well."

I think of the expense. I'm not sure what all this crappy insurance we have will cover. And this information won't change anything. I glance at Gavin but he just shrugs.

"I don't think so. We'll see how he looks at sixteen weeks," I say.

"He? You think it's another boy?" He smiles as he helps me lie back and fits my heels in the stirrups. "A mother's intuition is as good as any sonogram."

"It is?" I hadn't thought about what gender the baby might be, but I suppose I do often picture another boy.

Dr. Jamison feels along my belly, pressing in. He nods at the nurse, who rolls a sonogram machine up to the bed.

"This will be a transvaginal ultrasound, not a belly one," Dr. Jamison says. "You'll graduate to those next time."

I nod. I remember.

Dr. Jamison turns the sonogram screen so I can see. Gavin steps forward and takes my hand.

As the wand presses against me down below, I'm flooded with memories of Finn. I didn't expect this, and tears start flowing out of my eyes so fast that I quickly soak the paper pillow.

"You okay, Corabelle?" Gavin asks. He tries to wipe my face with his fingers.

The nurse passes him a box of Kleenex. "It's to be expected," she says. "Emotional time."

I'm not sure if she means the sonogram in general, or because I've done this once before.

The black-and-white picture onscreen flickers as Dr. Jamison moves the wand around, trying to find the right spot.

"Still can't make out a thing," Gavin whispers near my ear.

"He hasn't found the baby yet," I say. But my heart hammers, drying up my tears. Was I wrong somehow? Am I not pregnant after all?

I should have taken more tests. The one I took at Jenny's was old. What was I thinking? My face flames that all this could be for nothing.

But then he hits the right angle, and an empty space opens up. Floating in the black is a collection of white dots that are unmistakably a baby.

"There he is," Dr. Jamison says. "He was playing hide-and-seek."

He centers in on the fluttery pixels in the center and draws a square. A heart appears in the corner, and below it, the rate, 150 beats per minute.

Then he measures the length of the baby. All the numbers lining up on the side match up to nine weeks along.

"Everything looks perfect," he says, withdrawing the wand.

"Will you print one out?" I ask. I have more sonograms than real live pictures of Finn.

"Already done," he says, reaching below the machine. He lifts out a series of printouts and tears off the last couple. "Those are for you," he says, passing them to me. The others he gives to the nurse for my file.

I hold the images in my hand. It's proof another baby is here. This moment lines up against the last one, those first sonograms of Finn. I can scarcely breathe.

I should be happy in this moment, knowing a new little life

has begun. But there's too much competition in my heart. Grief for Finn, who should be here right now, excited over the prospect of a brother or sister.

And fear.

Stark, bone-chilling terror that I will have to go through everything a second time.

18

GAVIN

Corabelle and I don't tell anybody about the baby. It's not something we talked about or decided on purpose. We just don't.

She has Jenny and Tina, who know already. And her parents, who figured it out.

There's no reason it needs to be spread around. She's so scared, and when she isn't throwing up or crashing midday out of exhaustion, she wants to think about pretty much anything else. We don't change anything about our apartment or acknowledge a baby is coming.

It's weird, but it's almost as if the baby isn't real yet. I'm not sure when that will change. Sometimes I pass the sonogram tucked into the corner of the mirror in the bedroom and it seems like a strange dream.

I keep working long days, like this one. It's a Monday, and cars are starting to come in as people with problems over the weekend limp them over or have them towed. My first job of the morning is a Ford F150 with a bad alternator.

Bud and Mario and my friends at the garage have no idea this pregnancy stuff is going on. After seeing Uncle Ben and thinking about what my grandfather would want, I'm definitely taking at least one class this fall, before the baby comes. After that, who knows what will happen?

At least Corabelle will get a chance to finish her master's degree. If she ends up with the chance to make more money than I do, I can stay at home and play dad. Why not?

June calls me every Sunday morning when my parents sleep in. She's kept me updated on Dad's progress. He's been in more pain than they expected, so he's surly. Not that he wasn't before. But more so. June avoids him as much as she can.

Life feels like we're marking time. Finish degree. Baby born. Nothing can be decided until we see what happens with him. If he's healthy. Or she. I picture myself with a little girl, and that is one thought that can make me smile. A smart beautiful one like Corabelle.

But when I imagine losing this precious girl, my hand shakes so bad that I drop my wrench into the engine of the Ford. I let out a curse and try to reach for it. It's hung near the bottom. I'll have to slide under.

Mario's two bays down, diagnosing a Camry that won't start. Nobody else is around to see my stupidity.

I snag a creeper with my boot and drag it close. I lie back and roll beneath the truck, glad for the extra clearance in the undercarriage.

Damn, I can't get it from down here either. I roll back out

and stare down at the engine, figuring out which hoses I'll have to pull to get enough room to reach down.

Mario comes up behind me. "I thought this was an alternator switch."

"Dropped a wrench." I hate admitting it, but there it is.

Mario laughs and starts rolling up the sleeve of his khaki work shirt. "You need to get yourself together, butterfingers." He peers down. "You beefy dudes have a real problem." He snakes an arm down, shifting a hose, until his hand brushes the wrench. He misses, but the move makes it fall all the way through, the metal clanging on the concrete below.

"You're welcome," he says, withdrawing his skinny arm and making a fist to show off his rather unspectacular bicep. "That's why I don't lift weights. To be the hero."

I shake my head and kneel down to retrieve the wrench. "Don't you have something to do?"

"Making fun of your screwups is my favorite pastime," he says. He shoves his cap more square on a riot of black curls — that boy needs a haircut — and gives me a salute.

For a moment I feel some chagrin that I've kept such a big secret from my friend.

But nah, I can't tell Mario what's going on. He's a bachelor and wouldn't get it.

These long days will pass, one way or another. Everyone will know when it's time.

My phone buzzes with a text from Corabelle. I sit in the driver's seat of the Ford like I'm about to fire it up. But it covers for me reading her message and hides my face in case it's bad.

Feeling really sick. Tina is driving me home. We'll have to fetch my car from campus later.

Dang. She's really going through the wringer. But she did last time too. I type out a quick note that I'll handle it and start up the Ford.

Everything hums along as it should. I hop out and spot my boss Bud with his clipboard, motioning another car to drive into an empty bay. He's sweating bullets in the heat, his bald head shiny.

I stick my head out the door of the truck. "I'm going to drive this around, make sure the alternator is charging," I tell him.

He nods.

I check the clock. It's pretty close to lunch.

"Hey, Mario," I call out. "When's your break?"

He shrugs.

Bud motions for the car to stop over the bay with a pit. "You need him for something?" he asks.

"Corabelle had to leave her car on campus. I thought I might take him to drive it back while I test the truck."

"That's all right. Just hightail it back. Looks like it's going to be a busy one."

Mario drops the lid of the Camry and hurries over. "Call in a pizza and we can grab it on the way back," he says.

"Sounds like a plan to me," I say.

He jumps in the passenger seat, and I back out of the bay. Bud rolls my creeper and the toolbox aside. Probably someone else will be in the spot by the time we get back. It's fine. Despite the mishap with the wrench, I haven't screwed up an alternator yet. This truck is probably good to go.

Mario calls in his pizza and we head to UCSD. I didn't ask Corabelle where she parked but I figure it's her usual lot. If I can't find it, I'll check with her.

"So what's the deal with the car?" Mario asks. "Got a crap mechanic who owns it?"

"You're a real card," I say. But I'm not sure I can tell him the real reason. It will lead to questions I'm not sure I want to answer. I just keep driving.

Mario fiddles with the truck's radio, moving it to a rock station. Thankfully he likes the song he finds, so I'm off the hook for explaining things.

UCSD is quieter during the summer, but parking is still tough. I drive up and down the rows, looking for the nondescript silver SUV her parents traded us. I hope I can recognize it.

"You don't even know where it is?" Mario asks, his hands drumming the dash to the song.

"She always parks over here somewhere." I spot a silver SUV and head for it. Mazda. Nope.

Mario keeps mercifully silent as I continue along the rows. I'm about to pull over and text Corabelle when I see another silver SUV near the end. The truck rumbles that way, and yeah, it's hers.

I pull my own set of keys out. I have the spare. "You want to drive the truck or her SUV?" I ask.

"I have no desire to look like a soccer mom," he says.

I open my door and hop down.

When he comes around to the driver's side, I say, "Thanks."

"No prob," he says. "Still curious why she left hers."

"She wasn't feeling well. Not up to driving."

"Oh, sorry, man." He has the sense to look chagrined.

"Not a big deal. See you back at Bud's."

He takes off in the truck. Once again I didn't spill the news.

There's just enough of that paranoia in me that keeps me from saying anything out loud. I've pictured that baby girl now, and I won't do anything to jinx it.

19

CORABELLE

I swear my morning sickness just gets worse as I enter the second trimester. Most women find it's easier, but I'm don't. The next doctor visit goes fine. The Dopplers find the heartbeat perfectly.

But the sixteen-week sonogram is coming. That's when we'll look at the condition of the baby's heart and find out the gender. As the date approaches, my stomach just revolts.

I can't hold anything down.

The fall quarter has begun and I'm barely able to make classes. I haven't worked on my thesis at all. I'm not sure I will graduate in January after all. Everything is going to hell.

I've avoided Professor White. I feel like I've thrown away all my opportunities. He went out of his way to get me a scholarship, and an adjunct job I had to turn down. And here I am, not even doing my work.

The day of my sonogram, I skip class entirely. My body is wrung out. The pills Dr. Jamison prescribed to help with the nausea have not helped much. Even if the baby doesn't have a heart defect, it's probably a malnourished skeleton.

Picturing this sends me on a terrible crying jag every time. I just want this to be over. Tell me the baby is dead, or will die, and just be done.

I want it done.

When Gavin comes home to take me to the appointment, I'm lying in the dark of the bedroom, still in pajamas, a wet towel over my face.

He curls up beside me. "You okay, Corabelle?"

I can't even answer. Moving my head might jostle my stomach. I can't throw up anything else. There's nothing there. But the heaving is painful and brings on a debilitating headache.

Something fuzzy brushes my arm. It's flat with round edges. A pillow, maybe.

I move the towel aside. It's a rainbow butterfly, furry and soft.

"Thought we could use a little something extra today," Gavin says.

I hug the pillow to my chest. "I love it," I say.

"You want me to pick out some clothes for you?" he asks. "I'll probably go for the slinky red dress."

"I don't think this belly will go in the slinky dress anymore." I press a hand to my stomach. My hips have gotten bonier due to the sickness, but the bulge is pretty pronounced.

Gavin bends down to kiss it. "Looks perfect to me," he says, and heads to the closet.

My head is still in all the wrong places, though, and when Gavin comes out with an outfit, it's as if we've gone straight back to the day of Finn's funeral. Gavin tried to help me find something to wear, but my belly was still all pillowed and I couldn't find any shoes.

I wouldn't leave then, just like now.

My belly convulses as I hold back a sob. This is never going to work.

"I don't want to go," I say. "I can't bear it."

Gavin sits next to me again. "So not knowing is easier?"

"If it's bad," I say.

"But what if it's not?"

I don't tell him that I don't see any way it could be good. I can't eat. I barely sleep. Even the vitamins come back up.

There's no way this baby is healthy. Just no way.

I roll onto my side around the pillow.

"Hey," he says, brushing back my hair. "Let's not think about the sonogram, okay? Just the next thing. The very next thing."

"What do you mean?" I ask. "The sonogram *is* the very next thing."

"Nope, that's way down the line," he says. "First, I'm going to take off your pants." He grins at me and tugs at the waistband of my pajamas.

They slide off and he tosses them on the floor. "Picking that up is way, way down the line," he says.

This does make me crack a smile.

"Then these go on." He tugs maternity jeans over my ankles. They slide up easily. Mom sent them last week when I told her I was just leaving my normal jeans unsnapped. This offended her somewhat prudish sensibilities.

And they *were* more comfortable, I had to admit.

She took care not to send anything I had worn with Finn. The box of my old maternity clothes is still in my old room in the closet.

I'm not sure I can ever wear those again.

These are new, still a little stiff. But Gavin gets them up. "This stretch panel is convenient," he says, sliding his hand down inside. "Lots of room."

Now I have to laugh, at least a little, and slap his hand. "You already did your damage down there," I say.

"And I will do it again and again."

I sober up a little at that because I know we haven't been doing it again and again, not lately. I'm so sick, and so afraid. Every bump, every sudden movement, every time I trip on my own feet, I'm afraid I will hurt something and cause another baby to die. Sex seems impossible.

"Next is the shirt," he says, lifting the bottom of my pajama top. I have to set down the pillow to give him room.

The air hits my skin as he works it over my head.

"Mmm, maybe we'll stay this way for a bit," he says. His hand traces the underside of a breast.

I'll admit, I do feel a twinge of interest when he does that.

Gavin picks up the T-shirt. "Dang, a bra. Let me look." He looks at me, one eyebrow raised. "Or can I convince you to go without?"

All right, he's got me. My mood has lifted.

"Not a chance," I say. "At least not in public."

He lets out a big heavy sigh. "Worth a shot."

"Top drawer," I say. "The peach one."

He grabs it. "Uh, this is not what I expected." He holds it up. "There's no hooks."

I sit up and take it from him. "It's an athletic bra," I say. "Underwire is just too much right now."

Gavin watches as I pull it on, then I pick up the shirt from the bed.

"Can you get me a brush?" I ask.

He jumps up, relief on his face that I'm coming around. I always do for him. He has that magic over me.

"Let me," he says.

The brush makes my scalp tingle as he runs it through my long hair. He finds a few tangles and carefully presses against my head so he won't pull too hard.

By the time he's done, I feel relaxed and good.

"Ready?" he asks, kissing my shoulder.

"Ready," I say. I should have had more faith in him.

Faith in myself.

And in the baby.

I pick up the rainbow butterfly and take his hand. Then we're off to the car, heading to the doctor's office.

And on to whatever we'll have to deal with next.

20

GAVIN

This sonogram isn't in Dr. Jamison's normal office. When we check in, Corabelle and I are herded to another part of the building.

"We're going to radiology," Corabelle whispers. Her face is white and she clutches the pillow I gave her. "Some stranger will look!"

I look at the paper I was handed. "It says Level II sonogram on here," I say. "Maybe it requires a higher-level tech."

Corabelle's face is pinched and red, like she's going to cry any second. I'm not any happier with this turn of events than she is, but we don't have a choice.

We enter the radiology wing and I turn our paper in to the woman at the desk. We sit in a small waiting area with a couple women with bulging bellies, and a few others who must be coming in for some other reason. Many are my mom's age.

The wait is terrible. Corabelle has this glazed look, like she's trying to forget where she is and what is coming. She manages not to throw up or anything bad, though. I've secretly been folding up little trash bags and keeping them in my pocket to be prepared.

I haven't told her this, but in the time we've lived together, I've checked on the trash bags regularly. We never talked about it, but one time, when she was in the hospital with pneumonia, I went to her apartment to take out her trash and discovered a secret of hers.

She poked holes in the bottom of all her trash bags.

I have no idea why, if she has some thing about a kid getting in there and suffocating, or what. The weird thing is, when kids DID start coming around, after we lived together, and Jenny had her baby, and Rose sent Manuel to visit, she stopped doing it.

Now is not the time to ask about it, though.

The other pregnant women have gone back, so I figure we're up next. At least one has come out with a printout, on the phone telling someone she is having a boy.

"Corabelle?" a voice announces.

We both look up. It's a different person than has called any of the others. She's mid-forties with short black hair tipped in purple.

"Ready?" she asks.

I take Corabelle's hand. She hangs on to the pillow and we follow the woman through a hall and into a small semi-dark room.

"Just hop up here," the woman says.

I take the pillow from Corabelle as she settles on the exam table. The woman arranges Corabelle's pants and shirt to expose her belly, tucking some protective paper into the jeans so they don't get gel on them.

This view of her aligns completely with the one sonogram we

had of Finn. We didn't get the early one. I guess her old doctor didn't do that. There was just the one, around this time, to check on him and determine that he was a boy.

We want to know the gender. Corabelle's friend Jenny made a big deal about not finding out until the baby arrived. But both Corabelle and Tina took the approach of wanting to know as much as possible as soon as possible. Maybe that's part of dealing with losing your first kid.

I don't know that I hope for either thing. I have pictured a little girl many times since I first imagined her. But a boy is fine too. Just a healthy heart. All we ask for is a healthy heart.

"The radiologist will be in very soon," the woman says. She arranges the stool, the machine, and the squeeze bottle of gel in its warmer. Then she leaves.

"There's no baby pictures in here," Corabelle says.

"Too dark, maybe?" I say.

"Or it's a room where they don't want to upset the patients," she says.

I can't imagine they would have a dedicated room for women whose babies might have something wrong with them, or die. But who knows? I'm not going to argue with Corabelle, not now. That's for sure.

After a quick knock, the door opens and a different woman comes in. "I'm Shelly," she says, shaking both our hands.

She has short curly hair and reminds me of Tina. I guess to differentiate between her and the assistants, she has a white coat on over her scrubs.

Shelly sits on the stool. "So you're sixteen weeks, I see." She pulls up a screen and types a few strokes. Corabelle's name and information comes up in the corner.

She picks up the gel and shakes it, then leans to squirt some on Corabelle's stomach. "We'll be doing the standard measurements," she says. "Length, head, femur, belly. We'll look at the nuchal fold to rule out Down Syndrome. And we'll take a look at the baby's heart. Do you want to know the gender?"

"Yes," Corabelle says. "And our last baby had hypoplastic left heart syndrome. Will you be able to tell if this one does?"

"Definitely," she says. "It will already have presented. Did it get caught early last time?"

"No," Corabelle says. "Not until birth."

"We'll take a good long look," Shelly says.

This makes me wonder why Finn's sonographer hadn't taken a good long look. But Corabelle said at the time that many heart defects weren't found until birth. It was past.

But now, it's present.

Corabelle's grip on my hand becomes a tight squeeze as Shelly starts moving the paddle over the gel. The blips onscreen are a blur of movement at first, then they lock in.

I'm getting better at seeing stuff. The baby is more clearly a baby now. I can see the head and the body and bent legs. Even the cord is obvious, sticking up out of the belly.

The pulse of the heart is evident in the shifting dots. Corabelle lets go of me unexpectedly and covers her eyes.

"We're fine," I say to her. "It's fine."

Shelly doesn't speak for a while, and the seconds tick away like a bomb about to go off. I look at Corabelle, who is concentrating on breathing, her arm over her face. Her chest rises and falls in a deliberate pace. Maybe she's trying not to throw up.

I hold on to her arm.

"So the size is spot on," Shelly says. "Sorry to be quiet. I wanted to be able to speak when it was time to say everything. Here is the length and it's coming out to sixteen weeks, two days. So perfect. And head is fifteen four and femur is sixteen four. All in good range. Might mean he's tall."

"He?" I ask quickly.

She nods. "Yes, it's a he." She moves the paddle around. "Boy parts!"

"Another boy, Corabelle," I say.

She moves her arm. "Please tell us about the heart."

"Definitely no hypoplastic heart," she says. She zooms in on the pulsing dots and freezes the screen. "Here is the left side and here is the right. All properly sized."

"But..." Corabelle says.

"I'm going to keep a watch right here," she says. She rolls the arrow over the top of the baby's heart chambers. "There's a hole here that is perfectly expected, one that will close at birth."

"But..." Corabelle says again.

"There's a flap that should come over it when it's time. I'm not seeing it. It's too early to tell anything, and he's probably going to be just fine. But with the history, I want to keep watch."

The woman saves the screen and pulls the paddle away.

Corabelle's voice is tense. "And if it's not fine?"

"Most likely, we give the baby a drug shortly after birth to close the hole. If not, it's a small procedure where we go up through the groin. Nothing open heart. Nothing major. Nothing life threatening in any way. Often we wait until they are two. And that's worst case. Most likely this is going to close up on its own."

Corabelle covers her eyes again. I can see tears soaking another pillow.

"Listen to her," I say gently. "It's going to be fine. He's fine."

She tries to nod beneath her arm. Shelly wipes Corabelle's belly with the paper and tosses it in the trash.

I help her sit up.

"We're right here," Shelly says. "We'll do another sonogram early in the third trimester and see how he's progressed. I'm betting it will be all closed up and fine."

Corabelle doesn't say anything. I help her off the exam table.

I should probably be worried about this little blip with the baby, but right now taking care of Corabelle is about all I can do.

21

CORABELLE

I'm a nervous wreck, never working on my thesis but instead scouring the Internet, the university libraries, and anything else I can get my hands on for information on fetal heart conditions.

The paperwork we got from the doctor's office shows a diagnosis, and I look it up. Atrial septal defect.

Everything says what Shelly told us. It will probably close up. If it's small, they won't even bother to fix it. Tons of people walking around with this. Yada yada.

But I'm caught in some obsessive loop. Every time I sit down to study something else, or cook dinner, or vacuum, I think of another question, a new scenario to research. And I end up on my duct-taped laptop, reading CaringBridge entries and health forums.

Tina comes over a couple times a week and we sit in a vigil with our candles lit. She's hugely pregnant now. Her baby is due in November, about three months ahead of mine. The quiet time helps both of us.

We haven't even come up with a name. Gavin jokingly calls him "the potato." Which makes me crazy. I don't know where he got that idea.

I'm not easy to be around. I've made zero friends in my final classes, even though my last literature course is full of fun people who like to get together and talk shop. Once more, I feel separate from everyone with my growing belly and my debilitating sickness. Not to mention the fear.

I've taken to walking the path from campus to the ocean just to stand on the shore and watch the waves pound the beach. Beauty and power live there, overwhelming all else. It makes me feel small and insignificant, helping diminish the crippling terror that creeps over me all the time.

One day in class, Professor Sparks walks the room with his anthology of Emily Dickinson, reading from her works. He stands right in front of me as he tells me this poem, then asks me to write about whether or not it speaks to me personally.

"Hope" is the thing with feathers -

I hate him. I hate the assignment, the idea, the ridiculous notion that hope could exist without me to nurture it.

The idea that I should have to hope.

Why can't I just trudge along in misery and pessimism if I want to?

But it's my last class. This professor is also my thesis advisor.

I have to at least consider the one thing I'd like to completely ignore.

Hope.

I pace my apartment, the single syllable on my lips. Hope. Hope. Hope.

A thing with feathers.

It never stops.

I pause in front of the picture of Finn. If hope has kept so many people warm, then why do I feel cold? Abandoned? Lost?

Like Finn in his grave.

I have to lie down before my stomach revolts one more time.

But the word remains.

Hope.

I hate it. I want to relegate it to all the other four-letter words I never use.

Maybe I'll replace it with hell.

That sounds good.

Hell is a thing with feathers.

This makes me laugh. I picture Edgar Allan Poe's raven now.

Hell never stops.

Even better.

Hell keeps people warm…now I'm hysterical, holding my belly, laughing so hard that I feel a little crazy.

And of course, that's the moment it happens.

I feel it.

A kick.

My laughter stops.

It's time, I suppose. Twenty-three weeks.

I lift my maternity shirt and look at my belly. My hands feel cool to the warm skin there.

I wait.

Then it happens again.

Thump.

It's barely there. A tiny foot with little more than cartilage, swimming in a sea of fluid.

But it's unmistakable.

Thump.

Now I teeter between hope and hell. I don't want the hope. Don't want the crashing into hell that happens when hope lets you down.

But it isn't up to me anymore.

Whether I believe this baby will come and live with me, or I'm certain he will disappear into time just like his brother, everything will happen just the same.

I can't stop the actions that Gavin and I set in motion months ago.

So I have a choice.

Live in hell.

Or with hope.

22

GAVIN

Time passes, as it does. The fall quarter begins, and I manage to start another class and keep my work hours up. Corabelle gets a little better. The sickness is mostly gone, and the baby kicks regularly now. This helps her, I know. Even though Finn kicked too and died anyway, it's a reminder that he's there.

That he's coming.

They take Tina's stitch out, but she doesn't go into labor. In the end, the baby is late, and winds up being born on the same day as Corabelle's parents arrive for Thanksgiving.

I head to the airport to pick them up, as Corabelle is up at the hospital.

I hope she's handling things well. I pull into the cell phone lot and barely get the SUV in park before a message buzzes through. The Rothefords have their bags and are ready at the curb.

The gearshift goes right back into reverse. They don't know

Corabelle isn't with me. They'll figure it out soon enough.

I guess if my Dad did me any favors, it was to get me back in Deming and in Corabelle's parents' good graces before today. Because the way things were after her trip in the ocean, it was a little iffy whether they were ever going to really forgive me for ditching her in high school.

As it stands, when I park the SUV and pop the hatch, her mom gives me a huge hug and her dad claps me on the back. Of all the things that changed in the years since Finn, this counts as one of the good ones.

Her dad opens the front door then pulls back. "Where's Corabelle?"

"Her friend had her baby this morning. She's up at the hospital. We're going to swing by and get her on the way back."

"That's wonderful!" Mrs. Rotheford says. "A boy or a girl?"

"A girl. Tiny little thing, but so is Tina."

Mr. Rotheford holds the door for his wife, and she slides into the front passenger seat. "Corabelle was a bruiser. Almost nine pounds."

I shut the hatch and come around. When I get in, we're all quiet, and it feels like we're all thinking the same thing. How big was Finn? Nobody says, and I feel a deep shame, as if I should know this detail by heart, but I don't.

"Well," Mr. Rotheford says, "is she still puking her guts out?"

"Arthur!" Mrs. Rotheford admonishes. "She says she is better. Is it true, Gavin?"

"Yeah, it sort of let up in the last few weeks. She's put on a couple pounds, even." Finally. She was scaring me a little, so thin with the belly poking out.

"That's good news," Mrs. Rotheford says. She smooths her skirt and straightens her sweater. "It's chillier here than I expected for Southern California."

"Just a little cold front," I say. "It'll be gone tomorrow."

"I never know how to pack," Mrs. Rotheford says.

"You have two suitcases!" Mr. Rotheford leans forward between the two seats.

"Oh, hush, you old grump," she says. But she smiles at him. God, they are as corny as ever.

It's late, the streetlights lighting the damp streets. It rained earlier, and the whole world seems washed clean. I pull onto the highway. Traffic is light, and the Rothefords chat quietly about random things until we pull up in front of the hospital.

Corabelle is outside the main entrance, sitting on a bench. Jenny is with her, bouncing Phoenix on her lap.

"Is that Corabelle's funny friend, the one with the pink hair?" Mrs. Rotheford asks.

"Yeah," I say. "She had a baby about nine months ago."

"Adorable," Mrs. Rotheford says, eyes fixed on the child.

Corabelle sees the car and hugs Jenny good-bye. Jenny heads back inside the hospital.

Mrs. Rotheford rolls down her window. "Would you like up here?" she asks.

"I'll sit in back with Dad," Corabelle says. She opens the door and scoots in next to her father.

"Look at that belly!" Mr. Rotheford says.

"You look lovely," Mrs. Rotheford cuts in, sending a nasty glare at her husband. "How do you feel?"

"Fine!" she says. "Tina's baby is a doll. Only six pounds!"

"Full term?" Mrs. Rotheford asks. She holds on to her seat belt strap as I head out of the parking lot.

"Past due," Corabelle says. "Week late."

"And still so small?" her mom asks.

"Tina is tiny."

After that, everyone is quiet as we drive to the hotel where the Rothefords are staying. Our apartment only has one bedroom. Which we'll have to fix before the baby gets too big. I guess he can sleep in our room. We're three months out. We should probably buy some things.

We park and walk into the hotel together. Mr. Rotheford heads to the desk to check in.

"What time is the sonogram tomorrow?" her mom asks.

"We'll pick you up at 9:30," Corabelle says.

"You sure we shouldn't get a rental?"

"Mom, you already gave us your car. Don't rent another." Corabelle's face is tired. It's been a long day for her.

"Okay, darling."

I'm glad she's on board with doing things Corabelle's way. She's about to see firsthand how hard a time Corabelle is having with the pregnancy and her fear.

We don't stay long in the room. I need to get Corabelle home, make sure she's eaten, and let her sleep. Tomorrow is a big day, again. It feels like every doctor's appointment is full of angst, another cliffhanger in this pregnancy that already feels like it will never end.

23

CORABELLE

Sitting in the radiologist's waiting area with my parents is an experience. My father, in his infinite wisdom, has something to say about every detail. The notices on the wall. The hairstyles of the assistants.

He makes small talk with the pregnant women, asking questions about their due dates. Mom frequently places her hand on his leg as a subtle command to shut up, but the women's eagerness to talk about their babies keeps him going. They find it adorable that a grandfather is at a sonogram.

Then comes the question I always dread, but this time it is aimed at my father.

"Is this your first grandchild?"

The woman who asks it is mid-twenties, glowing, and obviously near her due date. She asks with such innocence.

And it is a simple question, the sort of thing you might say to anyone who expresses that they are expecting a new member of the family. It's as ubiquitous as "When is your wedding day?" to future brides or "How old are you?" to small children.

Dad falters, glancing at Mom for guidance.

"This is our second," Mom says. "Another boy."

"How delightful," the woman says, tucking a blond lock behind her ear as if she hasn't just shattered the joviality of our entire group.

Thankfully she is called back and we have the area to ourselves for a moment.

Dad decides to pretend nothing has happened, a common tactic when things are hard or awkward. "How is Tinker Bell today?" he asks.

My first instinct is to snap something like "We've been together for almost an hour. You already know." But it's the stress talking and I rein it in.

"Anxious to see how he's doing," I say.

We fall silent as another couple strolls in, tall and happy, holding hands. They turn in their paperwork and sit nearby. I glance at her belly, in the cute round stage of the halfway point. Gender sonogram. I wish I could be like her, happy and eager and ignorant about how things can go.

But I'm not.

My hands seek the rainbow pillow, but I left it behind, feeling silly bringing it along with my parents in tow. It's come to all the other appointments. That bit of fluff is literally the only thing we have for the baby so far. I know I'll have to shop eventually.

"Corabelle?" The same woman as before, this time with blue tips in her hair, calls for me.

The four of us stand up.

"You got a party goin' on out here," she says with a laugh.

"You changed your hair," I say.

"Matches the stars on my scrubs," she says, gesturing to the green shirt with blue shooting stars.

She takes us to the same room, dim and humming with the machine.

"Let me grab one more chair," she says, hustling back out.

Gavin helps me onto the table and stands nearby as Mom sits on the lone plastic chair. The woman returns with a second chair. "Does Dad need one too?" she asks, looking at Gavin.

"I'm happy right here," he says.

"All right." She comes over and arranges my clothes for me. It feels awkward having my belly exposed with my dad in the room. They hadn't been there for the one sonogram we had with Finn.

"Shelly will be right in," she says and steps out.

"Interesting room," Dad says, and I want to groan. I close my eyes, counting the seconds it takes for each breath to go in and out. I'm not as bad as last time, especially since the morning sickness has faded. But it's still stressful, waiting to hear if your baby is better or worse.

He swims in my belly like a wave rolling. I place my hand over him. He's not quite big enough that you can see his movements from the outside yet. But I definitely feel them all the time.

The door opens. "Hello, family," Shelly says and shakes everyone's hands. "You ready to take a peek at the baby?"

Dad rubs his hands together. "I know I am!"

Shelly shakes the bottle of gel and squirts it on me. The warm goo piles on my skin. She brings up my info as before and slides the paddle through the gel.

"He's definitely bigger," she says. She locks in on the head and the numbers pop up. Thirty weeks, one day.

The femur gives us thirty-one weeks, four days.

"He might end up being tall," she says, glancing at Gavin. "Like Dad."

My father chortles. "You should have played basketball, Gavin," he says.

My mom squeezes his leg. I focus back on the screen.

Next the belly. Thirty weeks, four days.

"This is all in range," Shelly says. "Let's take a look at the heart."

She focuses in as she studies the screen. I can see the pulse of his heartbeat.

The image zooms, and the four chambers of the heart appear.

I have studied sonogram after sonogram on the Internet. I've seen bad valves, holes in hearts, underdeveloped atriums. But when looking at a real live feed, I can't tell anything.

She zooms, prints a picture, shifts, prints another. This can't be good. You don't document a healthy heart. My heart rate skyrockets.

I hate that she always studies before she'll say anything. *Just tell us what you see!*

Finally, she pulls back. "Let's take some fun shots," she says. She finds a profile that perfectly delineates the baby's nose. More printouts churn from below the machine.

She types "Hi, Grandma and Grandpa" on one and prints it too. Mom claps her hands, delighted. They are all smiles.

But I saw how she documented his heart. I'm bracing myself for what's next.

Shelly tears off the cute shots, handing one to my parents and a couple to Gavin. She leaves the machine on as she takes the paper away from my pants and wipes off my belly.

"The diagnosis has to wait on your doctor's review of the scans," she says, "but they will be forwarded to a perinatologist and a pediatric cardiologist."

Tears stream out again. So, it's bad news.

She walks over to a trash can, presses the foot pedal to lift the lid, and tosses the gooey paper in the garbage. She turns to Gavin. "You can help her up so she can see."

I struggle to sitting and we all stare at the blips on the screen. She scrolls back to the stills of the baby's four-chambered heart.

"Right here is what is called the foramen ovale," she says. "It's a flap that is open while your baby is in utero and his lungs don't function yet. With his first breath in the real world, pressure in the heart causes the flap to close and oxygen from the lungs goes into the bloodstream. At that very important moment, we have a human who can live outside of amniotic fluid."

She moves the pointer to circle a blip of white dots that mean nothing to me, although I can see the heart chambers. "Your baby's foramen is present, but it is undersized. This means that when the flap closes at birth, it will not completely seal. This may be a big deal, or it may not. We won't really know until he's out and breathing and we can test his oxygen levels and hear that heart."

My eyes swim with black spots, and I feel like I will pass out. Gavin puts his hand on my back to steady me.

I can't speak. I feel like I'm the one not getting enough

oxygen. I suck in a big breath.

"Lie her back," Shelly says quickly. She opens the door to the exam room. "Can I get a nurse?"

The world feels like a funhouse mirror, going in and out of focus, long and skinny, big and fat, images shimmering.

A large woman pushes Gavin aside and fits a mask over my nose and mouth. The air is sharp and smells like a hospital. Oxygen. I remember it from when I had pneumonia.

After a moment, I settle down.

"There you go, love," the woman says. She's not familiar, wearing pink scrubs and sporting wildly spiked hair. The people who work here are really into their wild 'dos.

I just want to sleep, but the nurse takes the oxygen away and an even sharper odor snaps me awake. Smelling salts.

"Let's sit up now," the nurse says. "See how you're doing."

The world is back in color and normal shapes. Did I forget to breathe? Did my old habit of passing out when things got hard kick in without me trying? I can't do that now. Not with the baby.

My stomach grumbles.

"She probably has low blood sugar," the nurse says. "I'm going to go get some juice."

Gavin closes in as soon as she leaves. Mom and Dad also crowd the table.

"You okay, baby?" Mom asks. Her face is pale and etched with concern.

"I'm okay," I say. "I just didn't handle the news well."

Mom digs through her purse and tugs out an energy bar. "Please eat a little something."

I don't want it, but I take a bite to appease her.

Shelly still stands near. "Your color is coming back," she says.

"I'm sorry," I say. "I'm screwing up your schedule."

"Don't worry about us," she says.

The nurse returns with a little container of orange juice. "Here you go," she says. "You're looking better, though."

I take the juice and tear a bit of the foil. It tastes like a dream, and my body gulps it greedily.

I pass the empty cup back to her. "Thank you."

"No problem," she says. "You need to sit here a little longer?"

"No," I tell her. "I'm fine now."

Mom and Gavin help me off the table.

Shelly passes Gavin some papers. "We're going to send you a referral to the pediatric cardiologist. The office might give you a call. When the baby is born, he'll be advised about the situation and if he is needed."

"Thank you," I say.

"Good luck," Shelly says. "For what it's worth, most of the babies are just fine. Our bodies are amazing healers."

I don't answer that. Finn wasn't healed. He didn't even get a chance. A doctor like the pediatric cardiologist she just mentioned made that decision.

But we have our answer. And now there is nothing we can do but wait for the baby to be born.

Thanksgiving is otherwise nice. My mom does the cooking in our tiny kitchen. Dad insists we go shopping on Black Friday and they outfit a mini-nursery in a corner of our bedroom with a bassinet, tiny changing-table unit, and some hanging shelves to store the baby's first clothes and diapers and burp cloths.

We start our birthing class. Each weekly session is another increment toward reality hitting. A baby. Sleepless nights. Midnight feedings. All the normal things we might actually experience this time.

Maybe.

It occurs to me that I don't know a thing about handling a baby.

And yet, I don't study. I don't read baby books or anything past pregnancy. I'm stuck in this terrible no-man's-land of being pregnant but not expecting a real live baby to ever come home.

Gavin brings a freshly cut tree home to decorate for Christmas. I frequently sit on the sofa, staring at the tinsel and smattering of ornaments, wondering how to find any holiday spirit, any excitement in life.

I have only four weeks until the term ends in January. I'll be done with my coursework, but my thesis remains unwritten.

If I can rally, I might still complete it before the baby's due date in early February and at least be ready for whenever I want to look for a job.

But I don't think I'm going to pull myself together. Depression tugs me down. The only thing I really look forward to are the candlelight vigils I do alone now that Tina has had her baby.

Then one day Gavin comes home with a bag of supplies. He doesn't mention them to me, just goes to the kitchen to heat up some leftover pizza, and starts to unpack on the dining room table.

Card stock. Glitter paint. Thin wire.

I know what he's doing immediately.

Making the butterfly mobile again. The one we did for Finn that I destroyed after Gavin left me at the funeral.

Four years later, he re-created another flock of these butterflies in the trees outside my apartment in an effort to get me to forgive him.

He sits there, chewing pizza and cutting out the shapes. After he gathers a good number, he takes them out the back door. It's a warm day despite being December, so he leaves the door cocked as he sprays glitter on the butterflies on the back porch.

Gavin and I don't speak, but when he starts to spread the butterflies out to dry on the cabinets, I picture glitter glue permanently on the cabinets and hop up from the comfy armchair.

We don't have any newspaper. But I pull out a couple large garbage bags and cut them open. Gavin helps me spread them on the counters and one by one we transfer the sparkling butterflies from the porch to the counters.

When he sits down to cut more butterflies, this time I sit with him. I vary the size and color a little more than he does as I cut.

We stay silent as he checks on the painted butterflies, finds they are dry, and turns them over to spray the other side.

I come to a bright blue piece of cardboard and have to pause to collect myself.

The special butterfly Gavin made for Finn two years ago remains in my bedroom. I saved it from the trees so it wouldn't get blown away.

While Gavin sprays the back sides, I head to my room. It's not quite the same as having a piece of Finn's old butterfly mobile for the new baby, but it does have a lot of meaning. It's one of the links in the chain of events that brought Gavin and me back together.

Gavin's back to cutting when I return. When he sees what I'm holding, he smiles. "When I assemble it, I'll make sure the new baby can see Finn," he says.

"I guess we should name the baby," I say. "Any ideas?"

"I guess Thor is out," he says. "I'm also partial to Batman."

This gets a smile. "I'm assuming not after your father."

"Hell, no," he says.

"We should tell them," I say with a sigh. "Mom is threatening to do it for us."

"I'll call Mom on Christmas," Gavin says. "Soon enough?"

I nod. There isn't much else I can do.

We work until late, cutting and spraying and stringing the butterflies on the lines. I get sleepy and lie on the sofa, but Gavin works on. He seems intent on finishing it tonight.

And it's a good thing, because when I awaken in the wee hours of the morning, it's time to panic.

I'm in labor.

24

GAVIN

I wake in the armchair to Corabelle's screaming cry.

I'm up instantly, jumping the coffee table.

"What is it?"

"I'm having contractions."

"Real ones or those Hicks ones?"

"These aren't practice," she says. "It's real. I remember."

The obstetrician had assured us that Finn's premature labor was due to his heart condition, part of nature's correction strategy. But now I wonder if he isn't the biggest quack in the universe. I'm so angry I can barely see straight.

"Car or ambulance?" I ask her.

"We can't afford an ambulance," she says.

"Screw the money," I say.

She sits up. "I made it last time. I'll make it this time. The hospital is close."

Corabelle is right. By the time we wait on an ambulance, we could be halfway there.

"Can you walk?" I ask.

"I think so," she says, but almost trips with her first step.

No way. I pick her up, trying not to squish her belly, and head to the door. The keys are on a tray and I snatch them, leaning to catch the knob with the hand under her knees.

Then we're out. I don't bother with the deadbolt, just the knob lock, and carry her out to the SUV.

"Towels!" she says. "I'll ruin the seats if my water breaks!"

"Screw the seats!" I say.

"Please, Gavin. Go back in, get towels, and lock the door."

Everything should be Corabelle's way right now. I haven't forgotten.

I race back to the apartment, snatch a couple towels, and pause to lock everything properly.

"Thank you," she says.

I spread the towels on the seat, then help her in and race around the front of the car.

By the time I've pulled out onto the road, her breathing has sped up again.

"This is pretty quick," she says. "I must have slept through the early ones. This is definitely it."

I count on my fingers as I drive. We're at thirty-three weeks. A little later than Finn, but still pretty early.

The contraction passes, and Corabelle lets out a long breath. "I guess we're never going to finish a birthing class," she says with a hard laugh.

Corabelle does not joke. She's at peak stress, and I don't

know anything to say or do to help her.

I white-knuckle it at each red light, and run a few when there are no cars and no traffic cameras to snap me.

Corabelle doesn't complain about this. She has two more contractions en route.

I pull up to Emergency and race around the car. "You want to walk in or let me get you a chair?" I ask.

"Don't leave me until I'm with someone," she says.

I am not going to argue with that. We walk into the waiting room and I set her down to race to the desk.

"Preterm labor, thirty-three weeks, baby with a heart condition," I blurt out.

The woman picks up her phone. "We'll get someone right out for her," she says.

I hurry back to Corabelle. My car is illegally blocking the drive, but I can't leave her. I promised.

Thankfully, a man arrives with a wheelchair, so I take a moment to run out and move the car to one of the emergency parking spots.

My heart won't slow down. I'm on a wild adrenaline rush, angry that this is happening again, supremely pissed that nobody took her risk seriously. As I wait to be buzzed back to the ER, I want to smash something.

I race along the curtained partitions.

"Gavin!" I hear Corabelle say.

I turn and see her. They've already got her on a rolling bed and are hooking up an IV. Her pants are off and she's covered in the gown.

"Is the baby coming?" I ask frantically.

"She's only four centimeters dilated," the nurse says. "Lots of time yet. We're taking her up to obstetrics as soon as they send someone down." She pats Corabelle's arm. "Don't worry."

I lean over the bed, taking Corabelle's hand. "How are you feeling?"

"All right," she says.

She seems calm. Too calm. This makes my pulse race all the more.

"You're handling this better than I am," I say.

She pinches her lips together.

"Hey, talk to me. What's going on?"

"I can't feel him, Gavin. He's not moving." Her voice is casual, as if she has already accepted the worst outcome. Made peace with it.

Now my blood pressure threatens to pop my head off my body. I step outside the curtain, looking for a nurse. They have to act faster! We should have taken an ambulance.

Two young men come toward us. "Are you here for my wife?" I ask.

"We're from maternity," they say.

I yank the curtain out of their way. "Get her up!"

They don't lose their chill either. They are used to overwrought fathers. I want to tell them to hurry, that the baby is in danger.

But if it's too late, it's too late.

Maybe all our pregnancies will end this way.

Corabelle looks at me sadly as one of the men comes between us. They adjust the bed and release the brakes, then start pushing her along the aisle between curtained rows.

Another contraction hits while we're in the elevator.

"Corabelle!" I say, squeezing closer to her.

"I'm...fine," she says. "They're not that bad."

It's the longest elevator ride of my life.

Finally the doors open and we head down a hall. There's an open door ahead, and the men move toward it. When we arrive, a nurse in pastel scrubs is already there.

"Hello, Corabelle," she says. "I'm Katy, the nurse assistant. We pulled up your info from Dr. Jamison and you're all checked in. The doctor on call will be here any moment for an assessment."

She hums as she pulls the sheets down. "Can you move or do you need us to transfer you?"

Corabelle says, "I can do it." She sits up, and the two men help her down and onto the waiting bed.

"Thank y'all," the nurse says, her voice a drawl. "Let's get you comfortable. You want a hospital gown or did you bring your own?"

"We hadn't packed a bag yet," she says. "I'm early."

"That's just fine," she says. She opens a cabinet. "I'll hook you up with something not too crazy."

I want to tear my hair out. "She can't feel the baby move! Shouldn't we be doing something more dramatic?"

"We've paged the OB on call. He'll be here any second."

She's right. She's barely pulled a gown from the closet and turned around when a man strides into the room, tall and self-assured. His shoes ring on the floor. "I'm Dr. Petersen," he says, extending a hand.

I shake it automatically. "She's only thirty-three weeks, and the baby has a heart condition. And she can't feel him moving."

154

The doctor has the sense to look serious. "I hear everything you're saying." He turns to the nurse. "Send up radiology with a sonogram machine. Let's do a Doppler now. And prep."

The woman nods.

"Sorry I haven't let you change yet," the doctor says. "Let's see how the baby is doing."

He lowers Corabelle's bed and fits her thighs into the big leg stirrups they only have in hospitals. The nurse rolls a tray over, and he grabs a set of gloves.

I turn to Corabelle. She's still serene and cool, almost remote.

"She's still pretty tight down below, but with the contractions, that will change. We're going to inject steroids to help the baby's lungs, just in case. We'll administer some drugs to stop labor."

"They didn't work last time," I say.

He nods. "I'll page our pediatric cardiologist on call to let him know we might have a birth. We'll also notify the one your OB chose for you. We'll see who's available if the baby makes his arrival."

Another nurse walks in with the little machine that amplifies the baby's heart. She's young with perfect curls in her ponytail, like a Barbie doll.

"Hello!" she says. "I'm Adrianna, your RN. Katy and I will be taking care of you until seven."

"Let's just take a listen to that heart before I go," the doctor says.

Adrianna smooths a bit of gel on Corabelle and turns it on. The whomp whomp comes quickly.

"That's Mom," she says with a big smile. "She's a little nervous."

She moves the wand around.

Corabelle closes her eyes. I know she's already given up and just awaits the news.

But then we hear it. A heartbeat double the time of the other.

"Got a good strong sound," the doctor says.

He listens for a moment.

"Well, there is a murmur, but that doesn't mean much," he says. "That's very common." He turns to Katy. "Get that monitor going. Make sure the NICU is alerted."

He shakes our hands again. "I'll be watching even when I'm not in the room. You're in good hands until Dr. Jamison can make rounds tomorrow."

Then he's gone.

I feel strange, like nobody's listening. But Adrianna cleans the gel and Katy brings over a blue gown with storks on it. "Let's change you before we start adding all the straps and gizmos," she says.

"Should I call your parents?" I ask.

"Wait until morning," Corabelle says. She seems more in shock now than calm. I don't know what she's feeling other than hopefully relief that the baby is still with us.

"Okay." I drag a chair near her bed. "So we just wait."

"That's what we do here," Katy says, tying Corabelle's gown. "A whole lot of waitin'."

25

CORABELLE

Somehow, I sleep.

The sonographer says the baby looks fine. The monitors show he's handling the contractions like a champ. An IV drug is ordered to stop the labor.

I know it's not working. Every half hour or so, a contraction takes on a new intensity, rolling more deeply. It's going to keep going until this baby is out.

Dr. Petersen stops by again, reviewing the monitors and frowning. "You're right. You do not respond to terbutaline," he says. "We've administered the corticosteroid for the baby's lungs. We have also given you antibiotics in case there is something disturbing the membranes. Now we just wait it out."

I can't believe there is nothing else to do. Another contraction begins, and I huff along. They haven't given me a spinal block, assuming my labor would stop.

Dr. Petersen is polite enough to wait the contraction out before he leaves, patting my leg. Oh, I want Dr. Jamison back. I glance at the clock. His office will open soon. Hopefully he will come before his appointments start.

Gavin calls my parents. I talk to them briefly, just after a contraction ends but before another can start. I don't want to alarm them.

"If we can't get a flight, we'll just drive," Dad says. "We'll be there by evening either way."

I feel like an utter failure. I can't carry babies properly. I can't give them healthy hearts. I'm broken. I should not have children at all.

Despair crashes over me like a wave. All this work, the vasectomy reversal, the appointments, the sickness, it's all for nothing.

This was not meant to be.

How long will this one live? One week? Two? Until surgery?

I don't even want to give him a name. It's pointless.

I'm not sure which is harder to bear, the contractions or the rolling waves of despair. I close in on myself, refusing to talk to anyone, not even Gavin. I must simply endure this day, this week, whatever it's going to be.

I will never ever get pregnant again. I wish we'd kept the money for the vasectomy reversal. It could have been a down payment on a real home.

Sometimes tears squeeze out of my eyes. Other times I stare vacantly at the window as light dawns and morning burns on.

The nurses change shift. I don't care who they are.

Then things get worse.

I feel wet down below.

My water has broken.

I look over at Gavin. He's fallen asleep on the sofa in the corner. What does it matter? They will have to take the baby now. Without amniotic fluid, the risk of infection is high. Birth defects. Stillbirth.

I remind myself of these complications as if they are happening to someone else. My hand reaches for the nurse's button, but it has fallen down the side of the bed.

I don't bother to pull it up by the cord. It just doesn't matter.

The new nurse aide pops in. "How is Mama doing?" she asks. Her ebony face is cherubic and her accent rolls up and down in a singsong way. South African, I'm guessing.

"My water broke," I say blandly. "I'm pretty wet."

"Oh my gosh," the woman says. "Let me page the doctor to see if he wants to stop the terbutaline."

She pokes at her phone, sending a message to someone, I guess. I turn back to the window. Gavin stirs, looking from me to the nurse.

"Is something wrong?"

"Her water broke," the nurse says. She approaches the printout. "The baby is still doing fine. But this changes things."

The RN charges in. "Let's get her changed," she says. "Dr. Jamison is on rounds. He's going to skip to you in just a second."

So he is here. I find I don't feel any more comforted by my own doctor. He's just a man with a degree. The things that are about to play out cannot be altered by him.

Gavin grips my hand. His face is tense. "I'm sorry, baby," he says.

I shrug. "He got an extra week over Finn."

Another contraction arrives. This one is dramatically stronger than anything that came before. "Can I get an epidural now?" I ask.

"Dr. Jamison is on his way," the RN says.

The two of them lift me up, whisking away wet things and somehow changing the sheets just by moving me around.

I'm only just settled again when the doctor comes in.

"Corabelle, I didn't expect you here," he says.

And that's when Gavin blows. "We TOLD you we had premature labor last time. You SHOULD have done something to prevent this!"

Dr. Jamison nods. "I'm hearing your upset. This is a stressful situation."

He checks the printouts on the baby monitor. "No more terbutaline," he says, swiping through screens on an iPad. "The baby's already had a corticosteroid, good." He comes near the head of the bed. "Corabelle, how is your pain level, do you think you'll want an epidural?"

I feel like I'm the demon in *The Exorcist* turning her head all the way around when I look at him. "Yes, I want an epidural," I say, doing my best not to growl the words. I'd prefer, actually, to be knocked out completely. But at least let me not be in pain.

"Contractions aren't really progressing, but that might change now that the membranes have ruptured," he says. "I'm going to go ahead and request the anesthesiologist. By the time he can get here, we'll know more."

My eye falls on the little icon that shows the baby's heart beating. I want it to go away, for the monitors to be done, for all this to end.

Hope might be a thing with feathers, but it is a vulture, a monstrosity, dark and feral. I feel it circling but I won't turn my eye to it at all. My ability to cope is already at its limit.

The last damn thing I need right now is hope.

26

GAVIN

This labor is so much worse than the last.

It's not that it's harder on Corabelle. In fact, once the contractions increase enough that labor is inevitable and the epidural is set up, she sleeps through half of them.

It's just so terrifying. With Finn, we were teenagers and had this stupid naive optimism. We had no idea anything could go wrong.

This time, I know what is on the line.

Corabelle's parents arrive late evening, and she barely acknowledges their presence before tucking back down into her pillow. They gave up on flights and just drove straight through.

"Oh, baby, you seem so distraught," Mrs. Rotheford says. But I don't know how she gets that. Corabelle's face is a mask. The nurses keep saying she is so calm and collected. I guess mothers just know.

The contractions are only a couple minutes apart when the nurse comes in and says she's dialing down the epidural. "It'll be time to push," she tells Corabelle. "You'll want to feel it."

Corabelle's expression makes it clear that no, she does not want to feel anything. Her eyes follow the nurse as she approaches the little machine at the end of the epidural line and punches on the buttons.

I don't know anything to do to make this any better. You see what a birth is supposed to be like in movies or on TV, and it doesn't line up with what I've ever experienced.

Definitely not today.

I wish I had a magic wand that could sprinkle fairy dust over the room and turn everything merry and bright. The night nurse comes in with her holiday scrubs and candy cane earrings, and it strikes me that this might be the worst Christmas season of my life.

"Sounds like we're getting ready to push," she says. She secures the monitor on Corabelle's belly. "We're going to keep extra-good focus on his heart all the way to the end."

"All this has to stay on?" Corabelle asks.

"It does," she says. "Until the doctor says it can come off."

They lift the back of the bed so she's more upright. The big stirrups are attached in case she wants them. She doesn't.

Mr. Rotheford can't take the strain and goes to find some vending-machine coffee.

The first contraction hits after the epidural is turned down, and Corabelle immediately starts crying.

"Isn't it bad enough without hurting too?" she says.

"Oh, baby, you have to have faith," her mother says. "You have to believe he's going to be okay. Did you pick out a name?"

Corabelle shakes her head.

I bought a book of baby names a few weeks ago, but we never went through it. Until last night when we worked on the butterfly mobile, we had scarcely acknowledged that we were expecting a baby at all.

Her mother looks up at me. "Is the bassinet ready? The clothes washed? I can run home as soon as he's born and get it all prepared."

"It's done, Mom," Corabelle says, sounding a lot like her sixteen-year-old self. "I wasn't completely useless."

Her mother strokes her hair, fingers brushing out some of the tangles. "Okay, darling. That's good. I think it will be fine once he's here. The not knowing is what's hard."

She can say that again.

Another contraction comes, less than a minute after the first. One of the nurses stays down at Corabelle's knees. The other hovers by the monitor.

"You're doing great," one says. "Not much more to go."

But there is more to go. Another hour of pushing, in fact. Corabelle's dad wanders in, sees his daughter all splayed open, and heads right back out again.

I hold one hand and her mother holds the other. Corabelle's face is splotchy. She's quit talking to any of us, going into some zoned-out state just to get through.

Finally Dr. Jamison rushes in, his gown flapping and loose. He's wearing sweats and tennis shoes. He didn't have to come, I know, but he did, in the middle of the night, so Corabelle could have her regular doctor.

"We have everyone on standby," he says. "Let's see what

we've got."

The head starts to come out, covered in white. I blink and blink, because the view is so much like last time with Finn that I can barely keep the two moments apart.

The team assembles, two men and a woman pushing a covered crib into the room. I don't know what they expect, but for once they are doing more than I have asked for.

"Just one or two more good pushes," Dr. Jamison says. His gloved hands cradle the baby's head, turning it ever so gently. Then one shoulder pops out, then the other, and the baby slides free.

"Got him," Dr. Jamison says. He suctions the baby's mouth, and there are cries, loud and lusty. Everyone in the room visibly relaxes.

A nurse whisks away all the straps on Corabelle. For a brief moment, they let the baby rest on her belly.

She's crying hard, absolutely sobbing, her hand on his head, as if this is the only moment she will ever have. There is no reason for her to think otherwise. It's all she got before. Once Finn got wired up, we did not get to hold him again until it was time for him to die.

"Let's check him out," one of the doctors says and comes forward to take the baby.

"He's beautiful," Mrs. Rotheford says, wiping her eyes.

Corabelle's gaze follows the baby over to the cart, but her view is blocked by the crew assessing him. I stay by her side. We can hear him crying, loud and indignant. I would laugh if I wasn't so sure I might cry myself.

"He'll go to the NICU since he's premature," Dr. Jamison says. "But if he's stable enough, he'll just be in a regular bed there, and you can nurse him and do all the usual mother-and-baby things."

He strips off his gloves as the nurses work to clean up Corabelle and take away the stirrups and cotton pads.

After a moment, one of the doctors turns to us. "His Apgar is good, a seven. Excellent oxygen, good cry. Really, really good for his prematurity. We do hear a murmur, which isn't unusual. We're going to take him to clean up and then do a cardiac ultrasound just to be sure."

Dr. Jamison stands. "Gavin, you can go with them if you like. Grandma, you should be here with Corabelle."

He shakes my hand. "Congratulations. I'm thrilled for you both."

The cart starts to move. "You want me to go with him?" I ask Corabelle.

She nods. "Just like Finn." Then she's bawling again.

Her mother holds her close. "I've got her," she says. "Keep us updated."

I follow the team with the baby. When I pass Mr. Rotheford sitting in the waiting area, I point to the Isolette rolling down the hall. "He's here. Seems okay. Corabelle is in the room."

He heads to his daughter. I totally agree with his choice, although I wouldn't mind someone in my corner right now.

I guess I have the team, the specialists. We move past a nurse's desk and through a back door into the NICU.

"You'll need to scrub in," a nurse says, pointing to the washing station. "There's instructions."

I remember the routine, the soap, the pick for your nails, how clean they want everything to be.

This NICU seems set up similarly to the one we were in before. The bigger, healthier babies are near the front, some lying in open cribs, others minimally wired up in covered ones.

As you go back, the room gets dimmer and quieter. Those babies have full gear, breathing tubes, ventilators, and multiple monitors. Finn was with those.

This baby is nowhere that I can see. I finally spot him in a brightly lit room with glass windows. I'm not sure if I can go in there. It seems separate.

I stand outside. I don't know what they are doing, and this makes me start to feel a little crazy. Corabelle texts me to ask what is going on. I don't know what to tell her.

One of the nurses sees me and goes to the door. "You can come in. We're doing a short version of the cleanup. The cardiologist is on his way to assess his heart."

A paper has been affixed to the end of the crib with the word MAYS in big letters, then "Baby Boy" written beneath. We need to give this boy a name. I feel deeply ashamed that we have nothing to call him.

I have another son. He is mine, sick or well. Whether he outlives me or dies today, he belongs to me.

A nurse cleans him gently with cotton balls while an assistant sets a few discs with wires on a tray. How long was it before they wired up Finn? When did the breathing tube go in? The details are fuzzy.

But this little guy isn't weak. The room rings with his lusty howls.

"Getting plenty of oxygen," one of the nurses says. "Filling those lungs so he can tell us about it."

They don't dress him, relying on a heat lamp above him instead.

"Wait for Dr. Simmons before you attach the leads," one says. "He will want them off for the tests."

The baby starts to settle down, probably from exhaustion. He has dark hair, and he's long. His feet seemed oversized, toes splayed out.

I remember suddenly our second-choice name back when we were going through books with Finn. It pops in my head like a lightbulb coming on.

I pull out my phone to look it up. Seemed like it meant something we liked at the time.

When I see the search results, I know this is it.

I text it to Corabelle with a line of question marks.

I don't know where her head space is. She might still be disassociating. She might be asleep.

But she writes back quickly.

Yes, she says. That's it. That's him.

I glance around and spot a marker on a counter. The nurse watches me as I pick it up and write his name on the paper taped to his bed.

Ethan.

Meaning: strong.

27

CORABELLE

I'm trying to get free of my IV so I can go down to the NICU myself.

"You just had a baby an hour ago," Mom says as I struggle to get up and put on a clean gown to walk the halls.

"I'm fine, Mom," I say. I want to see him. I won't be stuck in my room again with another baby. Last time I missed everything.

I examine the IV still attached to a saline bag. They never took it out. I'm about to take the pouch off the metal stand and carry it when pretty much the very last person I ever expected to see walks in the room.

"Corabelle!" June says, rushing forward. She's holding a big blue bear and smashes it between us in a hug. "Where's the baby? Where's my nephew?"

I look over her shoulder at my mom. Why is Gavin's sister here?

She glances guiltily at my dad.

"How did you get here?" I ask her.

"We drove all the way from New Mexico!" June says. "Dad was so grumpy!"

Uh-oh. "Your dad is here?" I ask.

"And Mom!" June says. "We couldn't miss the baby being born!"

Oh God.

"Where are your parents?" I ask. Now I really have to get up. I lift my arm, pondering the tube. Maybe I can just rip it out.

"They went down to the nursery," she says. "We've been in the waiting room just down the hall. I decided to come here." She leans in. "It's after visiting hours, so I had to be sneaky."

I pick up the call button and press it. I need a nurse, right now.

My legs are less stable than I think they will be, though, and when they wobble, I have to sit back on the bed.

"I told you," Mom says. "Gavin is going to have to navigate this on his own."

"But it's his dad," I say.

"My dad does ruin everything," June says.

"Did you tell them about the baby?" I ask Mom. "Gavin was going to let them know at Christmas."

Mom's eyes flicker over to Dad again. "We just didn't think it was right, since the baby might be sick."

I draw in a breath to really let her have it, but she holds up her hand. "I knew you might be upset, Corabelle, but Alaina never got over not getting to see Finn before he died. I couldn't let that happen again. So I told them, right after we were up at

Thanksgiving."

"And again today," I say.

"And again today," she confirms.

The nurse comes in, the one from the first night with her perfect ponytail. Adrianna, I think. "Everything okay?" she asks. "I saw you had that baby!"

"I need this out," I say, lifting my arm. "I urgently need to go to the NICU."

"The doctor hasn't given me the go-ahead to unhook it. You're getting antibiotics in case an infection caused the early labor."

"Then I'll just have to pull it out myself." I start ripping at the tape.

"Just let me unhook you," Adrianna says. "We can put it back in when you come back." She squeezes the line going in and pulls it from the base of the IV lead. A small alarm sounds, and she shuts it off.

It's a relief not to be tethered. I ignore my wobbly legs and head for the door.

"We're going with you," Dad says.

"They won't let her in the NICU," Adrianna says, pointing to June.

"I'll stay with June," Mom says.

Dad draws my arm through his elbow. "Let's take our time, Tinker Bell," he says.

We walk more slowly outside the room. Most of the doors are closed, blue and pink mums hanging on several.

I try the name again in my mind.

Ethan. Ethan Mays.

It's hard to imagine he is real. I saw him only for a moment.

The baby is like a mirage in the desert. You're desperate to see it, and there it is. But you blink a few times, then it's gone again.

"Just beyond the corner here," Dad says. "I walked these halls a few times while we waited."

The NICU has windows all the way down. There is no one at the desk inside the entrance to buzz us in.

I walk along the wall, fingers pressed to the glass. It's my nightmare all over again. The rows of babies in their Isolette prisons, moms rocking in chairs. Nurses bent over monitors, checking stats.

I can't hear anything yet, but already my ears are filled with the helicopter sound of the ventilator.

My feet stumble, and my dad grabs my arm. He wants to say something about how I shouldn't be here. I can feel the words forming on his lips. But he doesn't say it. Stubborn Corabelle, I bet he thinks. And I am.

Then I see Gavin in a room at the end. I can't walk up to that room, as it's on the opposite wall. But it's glass on the side that faces the NICU. They are surrounding a crib.

I want in. My feet in their nubby-bottomed socks fly back down the hall. Adrenaline hits my veins and my legs no longer feel weak.

A woman is just sitting back down in her chair at the entrance. I show her my wristband through the glass. "My baby has been brought here."

She nods and smiles, pressing a button so the door unlatches.

I'm in, but I know the drill and pause at the washing station to hastily scrub down. My dad will have to fend for himself, because as soon as I'm dry enough not to drip, I take off down the aisle, past the rows of babies that blink with lights and hum with monitors, past a nurse shutting off an alarm, past rocking mothers and fathers camped out on chairs.

I reach the room and Gavin turns. A space opens and I see him.

Ethan.

A nurse opens the door for me. "You must be Mom," she says, her gray eyes kind. She's dressed in full scrubs, head covering, and mask. They all are, except Gavin.

"What's going on?" Are they taking him to surgery already? Is it that bad?

I feel faint, like I can't take one moment more, as though the floor beneath me is shifting just to throw me off balance.

Gavin takes my arm. "The cardiologist is here. They just took a look at his heart."

One of the men turns. He lowers his mask. "Hello, Mom," he says. "I'm Dr. Griffin." He's older than Dad, lines crinkling from his eyes and mouth. His short gray hair is very precisely cut, like a poster in a salon.

He holds out an iPad and swipes his finger to bring up a black-and-white image. "I have Ethan's heart here on my screen. I was just about to talk to your husband about it."

My dad enters the room behind me. "Grandpa?" Dr. Griffin asks.

Dad nods.

The words about Gavin's father being somewhere in the hospital die on my lips. Later. They haven't found the NICU, obviously. We have time.

"So, good news all around," Dr. Griffin says, pointing to the screen. "This is the foramen ovale. The flap is undersized, but it's created enough of a seal that there is no reason to intervene at this stage. We will send you a referral to come see us at six months, and we'll evaluate again. Probably if anything is still a problem, we'll deal with it around his second birthday. It's quite possible it will fix itself."

I want to faint. He's fine? They don't have to do anything?

Dr. Griffin shuts off the iPad and tucks it under his arm. "He's doing amazingly well for being seven weeks early. I'm turning this over to the neonatologist, but I don't need to assess him again unless they tell me he has some distress."

Ethan sends up a major wail as a disc is attached to his chest.

"He seems like he's getting plenty of oxygen to me." Dr. Griffin pats my shoulder. "He'll be just fine."

Now that Ethan has let out a cry, I am mesmerized by him.

He's lying there, surrounded by people, but no one is comforting him. He's all alone on that bed, the heat lamp above him.

I step forward carefully, slowly, the way you might approach a deer. If this is some dream, I want to keep it intact, as smooth and perfect as the still surface of a pond.

He is not encased in an Isolette, just placed on a little baby bed with low sides. I reach forward with my fingers. I'm not sure they will touch anything. He could be a figment of my imagination.

"Ethan," I say, and he stops crying. His arms and legs wiggle, his head cocked, as if he's listening to me. "Ethan," I say again.

My hand brushes his skin. He startles for a moment, but as he draws in a breath to cry, I say it again. "Ethan."

He doesn't cry. He waits. This is one thing in this bright terrible world that is familiar to him. My voice.

"Can I hold him?" I ask.

Several of the people standing around look at each other in their blue caps and masks.

"Of course you can." A woman pushes forward, holding a diaper and a little cap. She is in colorful scrubs like nurses wear, her hair plaited into a crown of braids.

"Let me get this on him," she says. Everyone moves aside for her, and the group begins to disperse.

She lifts Ethan by the legs and slides the small white diaper beneath him. "Let's hope you fill this right up," she says to him in a quiet easy voice.

The nurse fastens the diaper and slides her hands beneath him. "Dad, pull that chair over here." She angles her head toward a cushioned office chair against the wall.

The room is empty now except for this nurse, my dad, Gavin, and me. A hush has fallen within the walls. The noises of the NICU, beeps, whirs, and alarms, are well outside.

Gavin sets the chair by the crib, and I sit down.

Of all the moments that align from our time with Finn, this one brings me the most peace. The nurse walks around the crib, careful to keep the wire on the disc from tangling, and lifts the baby to me.

"Put him directly against your skin," she says. "He needs to be kept warm."

I tug on the string on my gown and let it fall open enough to give him space.

The nurse places the baby against my chest and draws the

gown over him, shifting my arm to hold him securely.

Ethan is warm and soft and does not cry. His head rests just below my neck. He takes in a stuttering little breath as my heart beats just below his ear, as though he is relieved finally to know something. It is the sound he knows best.

His eyes close. Time has stopped. There is only this small creature, his tiny breaths, and the rhythm in my chest.

Ethan.

For just a moment, I see Finn there. Maybe it's the shape of Ethan's ear or the way his hair whorls just above it.

Gavin places his hand on the baby, his strong work-toughened fingers cupping his head. My dad sniffs, rocking back and forth on his feet, his hands clasped.

No one needs words now. The hard stuff is behind us.

We have survived the worst.

28

GAVIN

It takes a good half hour for the nurses to get us set up on our row in the NICU. Ethan isn't holding his temperature, which is expected for his gestational age, but he only needs a heat lamp, a heart monitor disc, and a tiny tube of oxygen going in one side of his nose.

Otherwise, everything seems to be okay.

Corabelle sits in a rocker, unwilling to take her eyes off the baby. Then she suddenly jumps up and says, "Oh!"

"What is it?" I ask.

She takes a step away, looking at the windows to the hall.

"Your mom?" I ask. "Is she out there trying to get in?" Mrs. Rotheford hasn't seen the baby up close yet. Corabelle's dad is out waiting with her until we're settled.

She turns to me. "No, I forgot with everything. I guess they're lost. Or with my parents."

"Who?" I ask. "Jenny? Tina? I thought they were coming tomorrow."

Her eyes lift to mine. She looks a little guilty.

"My parents did something you're not going to like," she says. She sits back in the rocking chair.

My gut tenses. "What is that?" But I have a pretty good guess.

"Your parents are here. I saw June before I came."

Now I'm the one popping out of the chair. But the windows are empty. Of course they are. It's after midnight.

"Where are they?"

"I bet they are waiting at the normal nursery, not the NICU," she says.

Damn. I did not need this. Although I guess it had to happen eventually.

"So you're saying Dad is here too?"

"Yes," she says.

Great.

"You okay here?" I ask. Ethan is sleeping. The nurse said it would be a while before they tried to give him his first feeding.

"I'm fine. Tell Mom to come." Corabelle looks up at me with worry. "Will you be okay?"

I shrug. "It's my family. Anything that can go wrong, will."

My boots strike the floor with each step as I leave the ward. The other mothers look up as I pass. I should be more quiet.

But I am not looking forward to this. Only anger will get me through.

When I approach the desk, I consider telling the woman stationed there not to let my parents in. But my mom will want to come.

I just have to deal with this.

Once I'm in the hall, I examine the signs to figure out where the regular nursery is. We didn't pass it on our way. It must be farther on.

My anger rises with each footfall. How dare my father just show up here. He wasn't invited to my wedding. He isn't invited to anything.

But then there's my mom. Damn it. I do want her here. She's been through enough already. There's no reason to cast her out.

Except.

She didn't protect me.

She was my mother, and she let my father do all those things.

Corabelle would not do that. If I turned into an asshole and started cuffing my boy, she'd rise up. She'd kick me out. I'd be done.

Mom had not.

An intersection of halls forces me to stop and determine which way to go. I look around. A sign on the wall says "Nursery" with an arrow.

They'll be there. I can bet on it. They don't know premature babies have a different room. It's not something they've experienced.

Because of me. I didn't let them experience it last time.

They never saw Finn until he was in his coffin.

I start walking until I spot the regular nursery.

The hall is long and a window runs along it just like at the NICU.

Despite the hour, more than one family is standing there. Babies are born around the clock.

I pass the first group, Indian women in saris holding up cell phones to snap pictures of a curly haired baby held up to the glass.

And then there they are.

My parents.

Dad is leaning against a pillar between the panes, his face close to the window, as if he can will his grandson to show up.

Mom stands a little behind, her skirt almost to her ankles, hair up high, arms folded across her belly. She holds a tissue and looks like she's been crying.

Why didn't she stop my father all those years?

My feet stop without my telling them to. I'm rooted to the floor.

Mom turns and sees me. She lifts the tissue to her face. She doesn't alert my father, but watches me like I'm something to be afraid of.

Maybe I look tough. My feet are wide, arms crossed on my chest. I feel like a wall no one can get through to see my son. And I'll be that if I have to.

One cuff on the head to my little boy, and my father is done for. I'll smash him into the pavement.

No, he won't ever get that close. Starting today.

Mom stands a little straighter. She walks toward me. Dad notices and looks where she's going. He sees me and pushes from the wall.

Here we go.

"Gavin!" my mom cries. "How is the baby?"

I wait for them both to approach. Mom doesn't come in close, sensing I'm not up for a hug.

"He's fine," I say, my voice clipped.

My dad tries to be jovial and pound me on the shoulder, but I turn sharply to avoid him. His hand misses and falls to slap his own thigh.

"What's stuck in your craw?" he asks.

"What are you doing here?"

He takes a step back. "Now, that's no way to greet your father. After all I've been through." He looks at the ceiling, shaking his head. "I practically keeled over a few months ago and you aren't even happy to see me."

"No, I'm not," I say.

"Gavin," Mom says. "We brought some things for the baby. Should we bring them up from the car?"

"No," I say. The anger runs deep, set in my bones. I couldn't shake it if I tried.

"Is the baby okay?" she asks. "Is that why you're so upset?"

I don't plan to say this, but it just comes out. "He hit me, Mom." I point at my father. "He kicked me. Cuffed me. Tossed me around. He demoralized me and made me feel worthless. And you let him."

She presses her hand to her throat. "What are you talking about?"

"You knew," I say, but then I falter. *Did she?*

Scenes fly through my head. The garage. The backyard. By the car. In the driveway. She wasn't around.

But then a few more come forward. At dinner, while she put food on our plates. In the living room, parts of broken vacuum cleaner spread out on the carpet.

She saw. She knew.

"What are you talking about?" my father says. "The boy

needed guidance. He was a klutz and a screwup and dumb as a damn post. I had to mold his pathetic ass."

The women in their saris turn to look and scoot farther down the window.

"Do not cuss in here," I say. "I'll get you thrown out."

Dad shakes his head. "This is the same shit you were pulling when I was in the hospital." He shifts his stance, lifting his arm like he's about to make a point.

But I knock his hand aside. "You are never going to get near my son. I will not have you abusing him and acting like it's for his own good."

I'm about to turn and walk away. I'll get them banned from the NICU. Hell, maybe I'll call child protective services and get custody of June. Actually, she'll probably stay here without all that. Let them try and take her back. Just let them try. She'll be great help for Corabelle. I'll enroll her in school here.

My mind whirs, so I don't feel the pull on my arm until it nearly stops me.

It's my mother.

"Can I see him?" she asks. "I never saw Finn."

I glare at her. "Tell me why either one of you should see my son."

My father hollers down the hall. "Leave him, Alaina. Let's go the hell home. He's not worth it."

Mom closes her eyes for a second. She's struggling.

"Alaina! Now!" he yells.

She looks at me. "You are right. I knew. I was weak. I didn't know what to do. He was my husband."

My jaw sets. "He still is. So go be his wife." I start to turn.

She grabs my arm.

"No," she says. "I'll leave him. I'll leave him and live in California rather than spend another day without you."

Shock blasts through me, hot and unexpected. I turn to her. My dad is still standing by the nursery, hands on his hips, glowering.

"What?" I ask.

"I have the spare car keys. I'll get my bag and June's. I can get a hotel for a few nights. I have a little money." Her voice shakes. "I've had enough."

For a moment, I don't move.

"I will never choose him over you again," she says. "I won't."

I relent.

My arms go around her and she clutches at me.

"I've had enough," she says again.

"Come on," I say. "Let's get away from him."

"Alaina!" my father booms. "Where do you think you're going?"

I put my arm around her and we keep walking. I expect he'll follow, so as soon as we turn the corner, we duck through a door marked "family break room" and close it tight.

It's empty, just a couple tables and a counter with a microwave and coffee maker.

"Where is Maybelle?" Mom asks. "She has June."

"I'm not sure. I'm supposed to find her so she can see the baby."

"Is he okay? You haven't said."

"He's fine," I tell her. "He's early, so he has to be under a heat lamp, but otherwise, he's good. He's in the NICU with Corabelle."

"Can I see him?"

"We have to get away from Dad," I say. I don't know what to do about him.

I look around the room. It's actually positioned between two halls, so there is a door out the other side. A shortcut.

"We can probably go this way," I say.

The other corridor is quiet as I peek out. We've taken a deep cut around the path I took to get to them. The NICU is just one hall down. I duck back inside the room.

"I'll get you in the NICU," I say. I don't know if she's really going to leave my dad, but if she is, that's a step in the right direction. But first I have to know something.

I turn to her. "Did Dad hurt you?"

She takes in a breath. She didn't expect this question.

"Not like you," she says. "He never hit me. But there are things he has said that possibly hurt even more."

I gather her against me again. "Okay. We'll figure this out."

We stand there for the space of several more heartbeats, then I cautiously open the door again. Hallway still clear.

I'm going to take my mother to see her grandson.

Everything else can wait.

29

CORABELLE

We spend eight days in the NICU. Ethan takes his feedings fine, with a little tube of pumped milk assisting his nursing.

This is the part I missed the first time, his little chin working with his mouth clamped to my breast. It's wondrous. The emotions that flood me when he's there are overwhelming. The nurse calls me the "tissue monster" because I go through a box a day.

I can't help it. Every day is a miracle.

When Ethan can hold his own temperature without the heat lamp and has gained another pound, they tell us we're about ready to be discharged.

June and Mrs. Mays, who now insists I call her Alaina, have been staying in our apartment. As far as we know, Gavin's dad drove home. His car is no longer in the hospital's garage. Alaina hasn't been taking his calls. He can sit and stew, she's decided. She wants to be a grandma.

Mom and Dad decided to stay in a hotel all week since they didn't feel like driving back just to return for Christmas.

A lot of the NICU is getting sprung for Christmas Eve. Babies who were already close are sent home. We sit around half the day because there is a backup on paperwork. The home health people are working overtime to prepare equipment to send home with some of the babies, apnea monitors and bilirubin blankets.

We don't need any of that. I just have to bring Ethan to a pediatrician within a week to check for weight gain and do a blood draw, and we're good.

Mom, Alaina, and Gavin wait with me for the final discharge. Dad is back at our place, helping June blow up an air mattress in our living room for them since we're coming home.

It's going to be crowded, but Alaina plans to get an apartment nearby next week when her job transfer goes through. The grocery store chain where she was a clerk has a store here and they were glad to give her a position. Apparently she's serious about leaving Gavin's father.

She's a totally different person, as if a great weight has left her. I'm fine having her around. And June is the most devoted aunt. We finally got her cleared to visit Ethan and she's happy to just sit by the crib and let him wrap his hand around her finger.

At last the nurse stops by our spot with a folder full of papers and instructions. Gavin stands while she talks, holding Ethan on his shoulder.

I watch them while trying to listen to the nurse. Gavin shifts from one foot to the other, bouncing a little at the knee. He's wearing jeans and a dark green button-down. Ethan has a red and white striped sleeper with this crazy long elf hat. Mom picked it out.

Ethan keeps knocking it off. It's more cute than practical.

It slips again and I catch it before it hits the floor.

"You can read over these things as well," the nurse says, passing me the packet. "The main thing is to see your doctor in a week."

"Thank you," I tell her.

"Good luck," the nurse says. "Do you have everything?"

I glance around at the space that has been ours for eight days. "We're all packed," I say.

"Merry Christmas," she says. Then she tweaks Ethan's foot. "I hope Santa brings you lots of things tonight!" She waves as she heads to the next family.

Ha. We haven't shopped for a thing. Gavin and I already agreed to nix presents to each other. And everyone else will understand. Gavin did run to a store a few days ago to pick up some hiking boots for June. They have ideas for some short trips in the desert while she's still on Christmas break.

Mom picks up our bag and I fold the last blanket over my arm. I look around one more time.

This NICU is not so different from the one where we spent our week with Finn. I glance across the room at the almost-empty row of the healthiest babies, the ones who just need a little monitoring. They've mostly gone home.

Then I turn to the farthest corners, where the tiniest babies lie in their darkened Isolettes, ventilators whirring.

The families there have settled in for the holiday, covering cushions with red and green cloth and setting stuffed reindeer on the tops of their babies' monitoring units.

I pray they see these next few days safely through.

"You got the car seat installed, right?" I ask Gavin.

"All ready for him," he says.

I guess there is nothing else to do. We head for the secure entrance. A few heads lift to smile at us. Some are still hopeful they will be discharged before the day is over.

We push through the door, and I look back one more time.

They say a rainbow baby, born after the loss of a child, is the beauty after the storm. And I get that. Ethan has certainly brought a joy I could not have thought possible after the dark depths of my hardest years.

But I don't really want to think of Finn as the bad part, the black spot, the horror I had to recover from.

He's a child in his own right, a light that still lingers long after his actual time with us on earth.

And if there is a rainbow here, it's all of us. Me, Gavin, Mom, Dad, Alaina, June. Each of us brings a unique color to the story we've all lived through. Every moment, good, bad, easy, or hard, has led us here.

This particular day of my life may be my rainbow, but I am still eternally grateful that at one time, I felt the rain.

Epilogue

GAVIN

We are never going to get this place clean again.

It's Christmas Day, and all I can see is tinsel.

Mom and June went totally nuts decorating every night while we were in the NICU. There isn't a surface of this apartment that isn't covered in strands of silver and lights. It's like walking into a fairy land.

Corabelle's mother had stockings made for everybody. We don't have a fireplace, but all seven of them are strung on the wall. Or they were.

Santa came for all, stuffing the red socks with goodies and little presents until the wire wouldn't hold. Since Ethan woke everyone up at four this morning, we've been eating chocolate from the stash since before breakfast.

Corabelle's parents arrived late morning with a full dinner. Turkey, ham, casseroles, potatoes, pies. With everyone taking turns holding the baby, Corabelle and I haven't done much all day but be happy we're home.

Late afternoon, Tina stops by with presents, a jaunty Santa hat on her head. Corabelle gets a soft new sweater. Ethan a little play mat with bars that cross over and dangle toys. She even has a bracelet for June.

She jiggles Ethan in her lap. "Look at all of us turning domestic," she says to him. "We're all headed toward becoming boring old soccer moms."

"Not Jenny," Corabelle says. "I think she's gotten wilder."

"You probably missed the meme of her with Phoenix," Tina says. Ethan lets out a little grumpy cry and she expertly moves him to her shoulder.

"While we were in the NICU?" Corabelle asks.

"I saw it," I say. "I had plenty of time to surf in the hospital."

Corabelle elbows me. "And you didn't show me?"

I pull out my phone and bring it up. It's a picture of Jenny, her pink hair wild and flying in a way that makes it look as though little Phoenix, who is behind her in a backpack carrier, has a huge pink wig.

The caption says "How rocker chicks raise their young."

"It was everywhere for like two days," Tina says. "You seriously could not throw a rock at the Internet without hitting it."

"I bet she was happy," Corabelle says. "She loves to go viral."

"Actually, she was pissed they called her a rocker chick when her husband is making waves on the country scene," Tina says. "She's been working on 'damage control.'"

Everyone passes around the phone. June's eyes light up. "I saw that! Can I get a picture with her? She's famous!"

We all laugh.

"I'm sure that can be arranged," Corabelle says. "She'll probably come over tomorrow. She's tied up with family today."

Tina passes Ethan to Corabelle's mom. "I have something else." She digs in her purse and pulls out an envelope. "I was asked to show it to you all and read it."

I glance over at Corabelle, but she shrugs her shoulders. She doesn't know what this is about either.

Tina unfolds a piece of paper. It's thin and the writing shows through.

My mother gasps. "That's Robert's handwriting!" she says.

Now they have my attention. "How did Dad send something to you?" I ask Tina.

She holds up a finger. "I'll get to that. First, I read."

Alaina, Gavin, and June,

I'm not a man of words. Not good ones anyway. But I'm going to try to say something here. You left me in the hospital and didn't come back. That sort of thing breaks a man. Changes him. I'm changed.

So I wanted you to know I've got help now. A shrink here in Deming. He's going to work with me. I included his card so you could call him. It all checks out. He's going to tell me when I'm ready to see you all again. When I've got a handle on this thing that eats me alive.

This Tina girl helped me. She'll pass along messages if you don't want to talk to me directly. I get that you might not. I'll miss you at Christmas. But she promised to tell you all this today. So I thank her for that.

Robert

The room goes so quiet you can hear a radio playing in the

apartment next door. It's "White Christmas," which doesn't match since it's eighty degrees out. But it works somehow. Our world isn't lining up in this place either.

My dad says he's changed. I'm not sure I believe it.

Mom recovers first. "Thank you for bringing this, dear," she says.

Tina passes her the envelope. "I met him the night Ethan was born. He apparently tried to get security to page you all when you left him at the hospital. When they refused, he threw a chair on the maternity ward. This got him locked in the security room to wait on the San Diego police."

"Oh, my word," Mom says.

"Darion happened to be coming up to check on Corabelle and asked what was going on. He realized the man's last name was Mays and figured it had to do with Gavin's family. He called me. I'm on maternity leave from the therapy department, but the lady at the desk was willing to let me come talk to him."

Tina leans forward and looks around the room. Her eyes rest on me a moment.

"He's got some real problems," she says, "but he's going to try and get better. I found him a therapist in your hometown. Sometimes it takes something like this to make people realize they have to change." She gestures to all of us. "I hope for your sake, he does."

Mom's face is streaked with tears. "I'm going to go call him," she says and hurries to the bedroom.

"I want to talk to him too," June says and follows her.

Corabelle lays her hand on my leg. "What about you, Gavin?" she asks. "Are you going to talk to your father on Christmas?"

I shake my head no.

"You sure, Gavin?" Tina asks. "Because I get the idea that the one he's really doing this for is you."

Hell. I look over at Ethan. Mrs. Rotheford has him tucked in her arm, humming softly. Beside them is Corabelle's dad. His lips are pinched, like he really wants all this to get better.

Then Corabelle. She smooths my hair over my ear. "I'm with you, no matter what you decide," she says.

And she is. She's been there from the earliest days. She was the first one to know. The only one to save me.

"He doesn't deserve it," I say.

"Nope," Tina says. "Not one bit. But he's hoping to become the man who does."

I stand up. If I want to prove I'm more than he is, then I know this is what I have to do.

And I do want him better. I want that for Mom, and for June.

So I walk to my bedroom, where they're talking to him on speaker. They wipe tears while listening to him go on about the Spam he's eating straight out of a can.

Mom looks up and sees me, and she's so happy, like my entering the room is the best gift I could give her.

"Gavin's here," Mom says. "He's just come in."

The phone is quiet, and the only way I even know he's still on the line is the word "Robert" at the top of the screen.

Then he clears his throat. "Hello, son," he says.

"Hello, Dad. Merry Christmas."

"Thank you for putting up your Mom and June. I hear the baby is a real cute kid."

"He is."

"Sorry I—" He clears his throat again. "Sorry I didn't get a chance to meet him when I was down."

"He's not going anywhere," I say.

"I 'spect not," Dad says. "I sure hope I get a chance to see him sometime."

The room falls quiet again and I know I'm supposed to say something encouraging. Like "Sure, when you're no longer a raging asshole," or "Hey, absolutely, when I know you aren't going to threaten him with a wrench."

The radio next door has switched to "Santa Claus Is Coming to Town" and I remember Christmas mornings as a child. We had stockings, and Mom made us wait until everyone was up to open any presents.

The old man was jovial, pretty much always easygoing that one day of the year. We didn't have much, but we always had gifts. And that pleased him.

If I could look at the one day a year, every year, I could see a man worth knowing, one I could stand to have around. Maybe he can make himself into someone who is that version of himself all the time.

So I manage to say, "Yeah, I'm sure you'll see him eventually," and I mean it. We're all works in progress. I sure didn't deserve Corabelle for a long time.

Something is only unforgivable if no one is willing to forgive.

I won't forget, and I will always be watchful. But if he can do it for a day, then maybe he can do it for a visit. And my newborn son will get to know his grandfather. And maybe this whole cycle will get broken for good.

The doorbell rings, and I head out into the living room. We're not expecting anybody else.

Corabelle's dad opens the door. It's carolers, all young men between the ages of sixteen and twenty or so. They are dressed in board shorts and flip-flops. They sing "Let It Snow."

We all clap when they're done, and Corabelle asks, "Who are you? I've never seen carolers in San Diego. And certainly not in apartment complexes."

They look at each other.

A young man with dreadlocks speaks up. "We're actually a youth choir. We were told to come here." He hands her a scrap of paper. "We got a donation in exchange for showing up when you arrived home with a baby one day. Enough to send us to a competition in New York last year."

He shrugs. "It happened to be Christmas, but we were down with that. Some of us got nowhere else to be." He gestures to the ragtag group. "We're headed to the beach!"

They start to walk away, singing "Santa Baby" as they go.

"I can't believe it," Corabelle says. She's laughing and crying at the same time as she stares at the paper. "It was Albert."

"Who is Albert?" I ask. Then I remember. The old guy Tina was friends with. The artist.

"Albert sent them?" Tina asks. Now she's crying and taking the note from Corabelle.

I peer over her shoulder.

A hospital staffer will call you when a certain family has a baby. He will provide the address and you are to sing for them. Make it a happy memory. They've waited a long time for good news.

Our address is scribbled on the bottom.

We all look out the door. The group is still singing as they walk, hamming it up so loudly that some of our neighbors come out to hear.

"He thought of everything," Corabelle says. She walks back into the living room to sit on the sofa. "He was amazing."

Tina drops next to her and wraps her arm around her. "He sure was."

I glance at the picture of Finn. Someone, probably Mom, has already framed a small photo of Ethan and hung it next to his brother.

It might not be snowing. And the carolers might be headed out for a swim instead of sleigh-riding. And we might be pretty poor and our family going through a lot.

But we have what matters. One way or another, we've touched everyone we care about today. The baby has come home. We're a family. And that is precisely the beauty of Christmas.

THE END

~*´♥`*~

FOREVER

There ain't nothing you can say
To make me turn away
There ain't nothing you can do
To make me take my love away from you
Because I said forever
And that's just what I'm gonna to do

There ain't nowhere you can go
That I won't get my walking shoes and follow
There ain't nowhere you can hide
That I won't find you with the love inside me
Because I said forever
And that's just what I'm gonna to do

How could you believe that I
Would ever have the need to say goodbye
All those years ago
I said the words that should have let you know
Because I said forever
And that's just what I'm gonna do

There ain't nothing you can say
There ain't nothing you can do
There ain't nowhere you can go
And there ain't nowhere you can hide

The FOREVER song is a real song! Hear it at
www.bradwhittington.com/forever.

Lyrics throughout this novel by Deanna's author friend,
singer-songwriter Brad Whittington.

Also by Deanna Roy

Don't miss the other books in the Forever Series

Stella & Dane*:* Stella is ready to blow out of her honky tonk town when a hot stranger rolls in on a Harley, leading to a dangerous romance that upsets the locals and sparks a tragedy that will change everyone's lives. (Romance)

Baby Dust. Abandoned by friends and haunted by what they've lost, five women forge friendships to survive the death of their babies. (Women's Fiction)

About Deanna Roy

Deanna is a passionate advocate for women who have lost babies. She founded the web site www.pregnancyloss.info in 1998 after the loss of her first baby and continues to run both online and in-person support groups for women who have endured this impossible loss. Find her on Facebook, Twitter, Instagram, Google+, and Goodreads.

Learn more about the author at
www.deannaroy.com

Your review on Amazon is appreciated—it makes a huge difference to authors when readers provide their reactions to a work.

Rainbow Baby Dedications

♥ In loving dedication to my two rainbow babies John and Manuel and angel baby Angelita Milagros.

♥ For Angela, my angel here on Earth, and Lila Grace, the angel who lives in my heart.

♥ To Ashley Sue-Ellen, my heart is forever yours.

♥ With love for my 3 Rainbow Babies, Victoria, Daniel and Aric, thank you for being the rainbow after the storm, I Love You!!

♥ For Justin, the rainbow after my angel twin sons Cody and Shane.

♥ Drayklyn you are my rainbow after my angel Adam. I love you to the moon and back!!! Love mom Dorie

♥ My oldest daughter is a rainbow baby to her twin brother Austin Michael— Lori S

♥ For my rainbow baby Diana and the pot of gold she gave me in my granddaughter Noelani. My heart is full.

♥ For the love of my life, my rainbow, Maddie. Love you to the moon and back. Momma

♥ My son Jake is my rainbow baby, my beautiful gift of healing from God. I lost my precious Sam at the age of two and then four years later was blessed with my rainbow. I will always love you my precious sons, Evan, Sam and Jake. J. Brady

♥ For Rowan and Oliver. Our cups runneth over from chasing our rainbows. We love you to Luna Moona and back ~ Mommy and Daddy

♥ For Kenna, 4 mo was not long enough to watch u smile. Watch over your baby brother Jeremy up there. Love your Mom, Dad, & siblings

♥ To my rainbows Emmit and Brody, born after sunshine Corbin and angel Dresdin! I love you all - Cynthia (mom)

♥ For Emma, Ethan & Wyatt, my rainbows. With all my love Mama Bear

♥ Maegan Renee Grace (2001) is our Rainbow after our Angel, Maclaine Elise (1999), and both treasured by their parents, Greg and Karen Loomis and big sisters Jessica Dawn (1989), Sarah Elizabeth (1991), and Katelynn Marie (1996).

- For my Emmitt, the light to end my darkness, the beautiful rainbow after a storm. I love you!

- For my loves, Evelyn and Maggie, the rainbows after the storms

- My rainbow baby's name is Zoe Lee Joyce Kinsella. Zoe leaning 'life', Lee is a shortened version of my name, Joyce is my Grandmother's name and she passed away 17 years ago but is still sorely missed.

- For Jaclyn, my rainbow. Your zest for life completes our family. Love Mom

- Grace Elizabeth (rainbow dash) my rainbow even on my cloudiest day -- love mommy

- For my son Baby V, the rainbow after my angel babies, Harper. And to Bradley my little bean who kept me going through it all. <3

- For Ayden Michael, you are the Apple of my eye. And to my beautiful angels Aleona Mae and Adaline Michelle. Your wings were ready but my heart was not

- For my Rainbows: Alex and Patrick. May your older sibling, my sweet angel Fetey, watch over you always. - Mommy MJW

- For my rainbow baby mia McKenzie after my angel babies Leon and Morgan love mommy

- For Finn Andrew, the apple of our eye and the joy that fills our heart. Love always, Mama Jamie & Daddy Ben

- For Victoria, Daniel and Aric, my Rainbows after the rain, and my Angel Babies, Bailee, Peyton, Finley and Spencer, I will love you all to infinity!!

- For my miracle rainbow AJ, born between my two angels, Baby F and Baby T

- Eric is my angel baby, he's all grown up now. he is always a joy to us.

- For Lena Marie and Abigail Rose <3

- My grandsons Angel baby John Gearson and Rainbow baby Andrew Bryan

- For my child Amber Michelle, the rainbow after my baby angel - Mama Tina

- For my son Robert William Tremaine, the rainbow after by angel baby, LaTrina Renee. Daddy and Mommy

- For My Rainbow Baby Selly and My Angel Baby Mami Yadira Love You!!

- I love you my rainbow, Chrys.

- For Patricia and Paul my rainbow children who arrived after my two lost angels ~ Mama Mirinda Jane

- For Trinity, the rainbow after my baby Isabella, may she rest in peace.

- To my granddaughter Jacqueline your always in m thoughts and prayers.

- To Gunner Daniel Blaine Johnson my rainbow baby

♥ For my girls' Kasha and Jordana who after a molar pregnancy and a life saving blood transfusion are my miracles.

♥ To my rainbow baby, Rebekah. Even though you are now a mother with children of your own, you will always be my rainbow baby girl. Love, Mom!

♥ For Alex, Gunner, and Gigi who are my beautiful rainbows.

♥ For Christine and Matthew, my rainbow babies after losing Adam.

♥ For my rainbow Joshua Jackson after my angel baby Max.

♥ For my rainbows, Clarissa and Braeden, younger siblings to my angel Sierra Jean-Love you always, Mom

♥ Quenton David and Tatum Dayle my forever rainbows!

♥ For Jaxon, my rainbow after my angel baby, Bo, who made me Mama - I love you, Mama Kayla

♥ Bianca Ala-Sue C.

♥ From my angel, Marissa Tenille to my rainbow, Amora Marie, with love always

♥ For Brielle, Kayla, Mariska and Onyx, the rainbows after my angel grandbaby Ryan. I love all of you very much. Your Memere

♥ For my Landon Eli, the rainbow after my angel babies Owen James And Evan Joshua ~ All my love Mama Sarah

♥ For my sons Dale and Dennis, the rainbows after my angel baby. ~ Mom of 3, Becki

♥ My children, Brett and Caleb, were born after my angel baby Candace Brooke was still-born from Spina Bifida complications. She is loved and missed every day.

♥ Derek Brandon Maguire

♥ Daniel L Barton II

♥ To Luke and Joshua, my beautiful rainbow babies.

♥ Raylee and Leland max

♥ For our precious Mariona, our rainbow and blessing after losing sweet Mar. From mama and dad

♥ To my beloved children: Cherise and Diane who brought me such joy at being a mom. To my angel boy in heaven, who taught me about faith. To renew my heart, my rainbow babies, Gina Marie and David Michael. Just always remember that the more love you give, the more love comes back to you. I love you all, Always and Forever. Your mommy..D

♥ To my son Christian Jesus, one of my biggest blessings and rainbow baby after my two little angels. Love you.

♥ For my little rainbow girl Rebecca Lynn - PF

- To my rainbow babies Aly Nate and Kenzi. You fill my heart after the loss of baby S.
- For my children Jennifer, Jessica and Robin James , the rainbow babies after my angel baby Julianna~ Mom Pat
- For Carter Jason, the brightest rainbow after our darkest storm ~ The Juneau Family
- To Scarlett Jacinda, whose snuggles brought me sunshine, and who continues to brighten my world with her wit, talent, and perspective.
- For my daughters Maggie Mae and *Rainbow* Delaney Paige. My life is forever yours ~ Momma LonnieRae
- My rainbow baby's name is Sylvia ,my heavenly baby is Katherine Mary, thank you, I love them always and forever ,Heather oxo
- Sofia Mercedez
- For my rainbow babies...Jorden, Morgan & Hunter after my angel baby. Love your mom, Sonja
- In loving memory of Levi Andrew our angel baby. Tucker Glenn and Ava Marie we love you forever and a day.
- Katrina Lyn Pennington
- To my beautiful Rainbow Babies...Tristan & Katharine. You have brought so much light, love, and joy to my life. Love you Forever, Mom
- For Tristan and Katharine.... my Rainbow Babies. You guy's have brought so much light, love, and joy to my life! Love you bunches, Mom
- For my rainbow Elinor Maze, after my lost little Pinto Bean. ~Renee
- For my son Joshua James (JJ) my chosen child by God after my angel baby Wesley Michael.
- For my rainbow baby, Xavier Stone, who gifted me with the positive test on the due date of my angel baby. You brought the sun back into my world. ~ Mama Cortnie
- For my rainbow baby, Sam! You have truly been the pot of gold at the end of the rainbow - Mommy
- For my granddaughter Abigail, the rainbow after her angel sister Isabel
- Makayla and Majesta, are our rainbows after our angel daughter Kaedance Grace. Heaven has to be more beautiful with her there. Love, Mommy and Daddy
- For RJ and Rhett, the rainbows after my angel baby (miscarriage) and big brothers to our angel baby, Rhianna Justine, who was with us for a few short hours before her final journey to Heaven.
- Matthew & Michael Freed

♥ To my Moon & my Stars, Lincoln Andrew Niko. My "Rainbow" which shines the brightest of light and color in my life, the sunshine when my clouds are gray, and the only Brat Boy Hercules I could ever give my heart to. Ich Liebe Dich meine Bug.

♥ For my angel babies grace Lana angel Patrick Martin Casey ~ mummy Debbie

♥ For my babies too beautiful for earth, Ernie, Penny, Grace, Isaac and Esther. Mama, Daddy and our rainbow babies Alana, Brayden and Cecilee love you forever, always and for all eternity.

♥ To my twin girls who softened the edges of a hole left in my heart after losing baby Mathias. May their rainbows shine for all to see!

♥ For our rainbow baby Sawyer James, born after our angels Gabriel Alexander and Cassandra Hope

♥ You guys have rocked the world in these past twelve years. I know you guys are hanging out in heaven living it up with Jesus! Can't wait to see you my loves. Colton David and Axel Micheal, make sure you take care of your brothers and sisters please, you guys are the oldest and in charge! Missing all nine of you rainbow babies, not a day goes by where I don't question life with you or without you guys! Love from below. Mom.

♥ For my beautiful, smart, and sweet rainbow baby Hunner Gabriel. Mama loves you more than the whole universe!

♥ For my children Isabella Jade and Garrett Xavier-Howard Robinson, my rainbows after my angel Connor Blaze. Love your mom, Mellissa

www.ingramcontent.com/pod-product-compliance
Lightning Source LLC
Chambersburg PA
CBHW020324260626
47156CB00004B/1363